Wilson's Tales of the Borders

Revival Edition Volume 4

ISBN 978-1-9998312-0-2

Published by the Wilson's Tales Project, 2017.

www.wilsonstales.co.uk

Design by Jon Goodyer

Edited by Joe Lang

Cover illustration by Claire Jenkins

Printed in Berwick-upon-Tweed by Martins the Printers Limited
www.martins-the-printers.com

Contents

Foreword

In this fourth volume of the *Wilson's Tales Revival Edition*, we have again widened community involvement in rediscovering and retelling these historic tales of Scotland and Scots abroad.

Wilson himself died in 1835 at the height of his success, and didn't see what his Tales became. By the time of his death they had caught the public's imagination and were selling about as fast as they could be printed: about 30,000 copies a week, a huge number at the time.

After his death, the Tales continued without interruption. Edinburgh publishers acquired the title and appointed an editor to both write for and manage the selection of Tales from submitted works. In total, over 20 different authors contributed.

We continue in this style for this fourth annual volume of the *Revival Edition*. Volunteer writers from across the country have rewritten tales in more accessible language; and researchers delved behind them to set them in context and ascertain to what extent each Tale is based on historical events or the original author's imagination.

We have again worked with the Berwick Literary Festival and Berwick Rotary to run a writing competition for local schools, and are delighted to publish the three winners from this.

As well reproducing some of the original illustrations, we include new interpretations from Berwick-based arts co-operative 56 Degrees and a series of stunning new illustrations from Charles Nasmyth, artist and author of *The Comic Legend of William McGonagall*.

This year's original Tales include *Sir Patrick Hume, a Tale of the House of Marchmont*, a story of survival set in Scotland's 'Killing Times' of religious persecution. Both hard evidence for the story and living descendants of those involved can still be found in the area.

The Trials of the Rev Samuel Austin is also based on the Killing Times and gives a harrowing account of the persecution and displacement of a preacher loyal to the Covenanter cause.

Three tales are imaginative rather than historic. *Judith the Egyptian, or the Fate of the Heir of Riccon* claims to be based on a Border Ballad, though we suspect the ballad in question is from Wilson's own pen. Set on the banks of the Tweed, it's a classic Borders Tale involving rival lovers and a gypsy beauty. *Kate Kennedy* is a more light-hearted Tale that sees a feisty daughter outwit her father's enemies and end a long-running feud. And *The Domestic Griefs of Gustavus M'Iver* is a farcical Tale of domestic mishaps, following similar lines to Shakespeare's *The Taming of the Shrew*, except that everything the long-suffering husband does to improve his marital situation simply makes matters worse.

Finally, we have *Thomas of Chartres*. The original Tale described William Wallace's journey to France to secure support, chronicling his adventures with pirates, outlawed crusader knights, wild animals and deserted damsels *en route*. Here, Nick Jones has rewritten it into a somewhat more modern context. Evidence for the original Tale is sketchy. There were reports from the English Ambassador at the French Court that Wallace was in Paris, and Thomas of Chartres did make a financial contribution to Robert the Bruce's tomb, so there does seem to have been actual historic contact between the characters involved. But the liberties Nick takes with Wilson's original may not be much greater than the liberties Wilson took with the historical facts. Read Keith Ryan's background piece, and judge for yourself!

But first, we continue *Who was Wilson?*, our 'Tale of the Tales', with an account of Wilson's movements and career as he returned to Berwick to take up the editorship of the *Berwick Advertiser*.

Andrew Ayre

Who was Wilson?

'Powerful magnets' draw him home

Andrew Ayre continues his history of Wilson and his Tales as Wilson returns home to Berwick and takes up the editorship of the *Berwick Advertiser.*

In Volume 3, we left Wilson living in Manchester in 1832. We know he was there in February 1832, from his surviving correspondence with a lifelong friend: James Everett, a Methodist preacher also settled in Manchester at that time. This correspondence, held by the National Library of Scotland (Ref MS 11000, folio 77.257-68), gives a fascinating insight into Wilson's character and the trials and tribulations of his life in this period.

We don't know much about Everett; he possibly came from Berwick, as he had a brother based there and his friendship with Wilson could well have originated there. He had become a well-known Methodist preacher, had connections in the book trade and was perhaps a bookseller himself.

The first of the letters shows that Wilson is still trying to get work published through London agents. He tells Everett that he needs to go in person to try and promote his work. However, "on the cheapest calculation which I can make, I find it would require about two pounds more than I am in possession of". He goes on to request a loan for the sum, explaining: "I would have called in, but I could not, it is with pain I have written this, and spoken it, I could not".

He also tells his friend he has had an offer to go back to Berwick to edit the *Berwick Advertiser*. This clearly has huge appeal: "The prospect which that situation holds out of being always at home, having a certain income and independence, with a large portion of literary leisure, makes me tenfold more anxious to embrace the offer than ever I was to obtain anything on this earth".

Everett lent him the money, and he went to London to try and secure the sale of his works before heading up to Berwick. But his efforts were without success and he found everyone unwilling to commit until 'the settlement of the reform question'. This was the big political hot potato of the day, concerning the reform of the electoral system to give broader and fairer representation; it was eventually settled by the Great Reform Act of 1832. It raised passionate opinions, much as Brexit or Scottish independence do in this age, and Wilson was a great campaigner for reform. But at this point, he felt, "the principal writers are of necessity resting upon their oars".

He returned with no more money than he set off with. True, he had three offers for "when the state of things justifies it" and one for "next season". But, Wilson commented, "this is as useless and profitless of hope to me as preaching repentance to a dead man".

His letter of 26 February tells us he needs to be in Berwick in about a fortnight, but "it would cost me much labour to do that as we shall have to walk to Newcastle", the 'we' suggesting that his wife is with him. He mentions a plan to stop in Leeds to give his lectures *en route*, and indeed the Leeds Mercury of 10 March 1832 reported a two-hour address to the Leeds Temperance Society on the benefits of such societies. This was something of a departure: his usual subject matter had been poetry, and there are many regional newspaper reports of his successful lectures on this subject in the immediately previous years.

to the United States they are little more than respectable;
but the recommendation that I could take with me I do not
think I would be long in finding an Editorship, and if I once
had one I should take care to — the — a short time in being
both proprietor and Editor of an American Newspaper. As like
the Canadas or the States are now peopled, this would not be —
myself, and in point of talent I would not have the competition to
—tithed with that I have in this country, neither is patronage
here an overshadowing weed. It therefore nothing better cast
up between this and that time twelvemonths, and I — the blessing
of health till then, I believe I shall try my fortune beyond the
Atlantic. Meantime let me have your opinion thereon.

I had almost forgot to tell you, that within these few
weeks I have received very complimentary letters respecting the
"Enthusiast" from H. R. the Duke of Sussex, old Earl Spencer, the Earl
of Saunterville Lord Hanick, Sir Rufane Donkin and others —
Mrs Wilson joins me in kindest remembrance and esteem
and in like manner remember us both to Mrs Everett —
I have not room to add more — Write immediately —
and believe me Dear Everett faithfully Yours
[Maria Theresa was superb] Wm Mackay Wilson

Mr James Everett,
Bookseller, Market Street
Manchester

Wilson received another job offer, to be editor of the *Manchester Chronicle*: probably a better job, but he felt obliged to honour his acceptance of the *Advertiser's* offer. He clearly also relished the opportunity to get back to his home town, commenting: "Health and home are powerful magnets to draw me to the north and keep me there".

Wilson did not write again till November 1832. Rather frustratingly, this time he wrote from the *Advertiser* office rather than his home address, so as yet we don't know where he might have been living in Berwick. Quite possibly it was somewhere in Tweedmouth, his place of birth and burial.

The reason for this delay in writing was illness. In the November letter Wilson indicates that Everett would have known he was ill when he left Manchester, and that it had grown so much worse that for several months after his arrival in Berwick he could not walk across a room or lie on one side: "Every person thought I was dying but myself".

However, by November he has recovered and seems to be making a good job of his editorship of the paper, which he had found in "miserable condition" when he took it over. Wilson reports that he has secured about 100 extra subscribers and that circulation is now as high as it has ever been in the paper's 25-year history. He also complains that despite the improved profitability, he cannot persuade the owners to invest in the paper, though they do seem to be leaving him with editorial freedom.

Wilson is grateful for his recovery and his new enjoyment of life, particularly as he reports that some 260 people have died in Berwick during the year from an outbreak of cholera. He also apologises that he is not yet in a position to repay his debt, as he is still awaiting payment from London!

In 1833 Wilson seems to have given up waiting for London publishers to come good, and self-publishes his poem *The Enthusiast.* His subsequent letters tell us it has been well received; he is having difficulty in distributing it and in getting paid, but is hopeful as the sales have all gone to "respectable" customers.

Wilson reports he is very comfortable in Berwick but that the available periodicals are old, books hard to come by and the library "full of trash". Now, being settled for the first time in his life, he seems keen to start building a library of his own. In April 1834 he joyfully writes of buying at auction a 1611 folio edition of Barker's *Black Letter Bible*. He begs Everett not to pity his bibliomania, explaining he would "rather want victuals for a day than a book that I desire".

Times were hard in Berwick, though. Wilson reports that money is scarcely to be seen, indeed, "invisible". He seems to have had difficulty getting his own salary paid, complaining in his 1 January 1834 letter that "the Humbugs have jerked me this year and not paid me yet".

As his health improved he went walking in the country. He tells of a walk in the Cheviots when he got lost in low cloud: meaning to find his way back to Wooler, he found himself in Scotland. His description of the cloud hanging on hills and enveloping him evokes similar phrases used in his tale *The Vacant Chair*, which he published at this time and which later became the first of his *Tales of the Borders*.

Wilson seemed to sense that he needed to move on from the *Advertiser*. He toyed with the idea of emigrating to America or Canada, and with offers to take on *The Border Magazine*, which had run into financial difficulties. He even considered training in law, but did not feel the financial sacrifice would be fair on his wife, particularly as there would be no certainty of work at the end of five years' training.

There was, however, an increasingly pressing reason to consider other options: the expected return of the *Advertiser* proprietor's son Henry from his education in Edinburgh. The plan was to install him as manager of the paper, which would undoubtedly cramp Wilson's independence and perhaps leave no place for him. But more of that in our next volume…

Sir Patrick Hume

A Tale of the House of Marchmont

Sir Patrick Hume was a lover of freedom and country when it was dangerous to be either, under Charles II. In 1665, aged 24, he was elected to the Scottish Parliament as representative for Berwickshire. Parliaments then were seen as weak and servile, and expected to meet the arbitrary demands of Charles for men and money; Hume, as an advocate of religious and civil liberty, objected.

"What!" he said to Parliament. "Are we only here to please the King? We're here to represent the people of Scotland, their wants and wishes, and defend their rights. Are we going to drag them from their plough in the valley or sheep in the hills at a royal nod? Are we going to tax their cattle and their corn and their coffers just because the King wants to? Stop and think. If we don't agree, he can't do it."

The royalist Duke of Lauderdale shouted: "Treason! I denounce Sir Patrick Hume as a dangerous man, a plotter against the life and dignity of our sovereign lord."

Patrick looked straight at the Duke as he spoke: "Though there may be a slave among us who would sell his country for a royal smile, I hope this is still a free parliament, and it concerns all the members to be free in what concerns our nation".

Already a marked man, Patrick was among those who resisted two years later when Charles tried force to get his way in Scotland. Resistance failed and Patrick spent the next two years as a prisoner in Stirling Castle.

Free again, he became involved with the 'incorruptible' Algernon Sydney, Lord Russell, and Mr Baillie of Jerviswoode among others to free Scotland from Charles by constitutional means. But at a time of real and imagined plots to dethrone or kill the Catholic King that kept informers and executioners busy, Patrick and the others failed to act together. Accused of a Protestant plot, a price was put on their heads. Some managed to get abroad, some took to the hills, and Russell died on the scaffold.

But in the autumn of 1684 Patrick, bravely or unwisely, was still at home. That changed on a September night when Jamie Winter, a joiner on Polwarth Estate, arrived breathless and frightened at Redbraes Castle and insisted that he must see Sir Patrick in private.

Patrick sent his younger children from the room, but kept his wife and 12-year-old daughter Grizel by his side. He said: "You've got bad news, Jamie, but you can tell us now. It's right that my wife should hear, and I keep no secrets from my little secretary."

"God bless her," said Jamie. "She's as clever as she's bonny. But you're right, I've got bad news. Troops arrived in Berwick this morning and they'll be at Redbraes and Jerviswoode before midnight. I heard the talk about a price on your head and slipped out of town straight away without talking to anybody. You haven't much time to save yourself."

"Go now!" his wife pleaded.

"There's no chance of that, my lady," said Jamie. "There are government spies at every turn of the road, in every house in the country, even in this house. Our only hope is to hide Sir Patrick here, but how or where is beyond me."

It was beyond all three adults for the next hour. Then, with time running out, Grizel, who had listened but stayed silent, flung her arms round Patrick's neck and whispered: 'I know a place that the King's troopers and his spies will never find, the family vault in the aisle below Polwarth Kirk. The entrance is small and long grass and weeds hide it. Nobody would think of looking for you there."

"You've got more sense than the rest of us put together," said Jamie. "The aisle is the very place. I'll get a bed and some necessaries if you'll slip away and join me as soon as possible, Sir Patrick."

Patrick was in the cold, dark aisle within an hour, alone on a rudimentary bed. The night passed slowly and at times he heard curses and the trampling of hooves in the churchyard as troopers searched. Kneeling on the cold, damp floor, surrounded by the bones of his forefathers, he prayed silently for God to protect his family and save his country. Then he slept.

Polwath Church

Daylight came only dimly through the small, hidden entrance, although enough to show the horrors of where he was hiding. Darkness fell again. Another day passed and his food supply was almost gone when at midnight he heard a rustle at the entrance and the piece of old gravestone covering it moved.

He heard a whisper: "Father! Father! It's me, your own Grizel".

"My matchless child!" said Patrick, stretching his hands upwards and taking her into his arms.

Sitting on the bed, she gave him details of the search made by the troopers and how everyone in Redbraes was watched, including what they did with food.

"But I managed to get some out of the house without them knowing," she said. "While I've got food my father won't go hungry. Here's a flask of wine, cakes, and a sheep's head. And there's a story about that head…

"It was put on a plate for me at dinnertime, and when the servant was out of the room I whipped it into my apron. When little Sandy turned round to ask for a piece it was gone. He couldn't believe it. He turned to mother and said: 'Ah, Mother, our Grizzy has swallowed a sheep's head in an instant, bones and all'. 'Wheesht,' said Mother, 'you'll get the next one.' But Sandy shook his little knife at me: 'Oh, you greedy Grizzy, I'll mind you for this'."

She laughed. "I'm sure he'll never forget it. I managed to slip out to hide the head in my room, then tonight I crept out the window to get here. The troopers aren't about the house now, and I'll come every night."

Patrick laughed at her ingenuity and bravery as he cuddled her. As he stayed in the cheerless vault for weeks, his only companion a copy of Buchanan's *Psalms*, her cheerful company for an hour or two each day was his only relief.

The hiding place was threatened only once, when boys were playing in the churchyard and their ball slipped through a small gap at the entrance. As Patrick braced himself and the boys dared each other to be first down the hole, the gravedigger shouted at them: "What are you doing? Do you want the ghosts of the old Humes about your ears?"

Grumbling, the old man moved the stone back. He muttered to himself: "Sorrow take the hands of those that moved it. But it's hardly worth covering up again, there's no money in it for me. The next Hume that should be in it will probably go the same way as his friend Baillie, who died on the scaffold yesterday. Gravedigging's not much of a job in this king's reign: it all goes to the public executioner."

Patrick knew he had to move, and left the vault that night with Grizel. Disguised and claiming to be a surgeon, he managed to get to London with his family and then to France. From there he led a Protestant attempt to dethrone James, crowned king after the death of his brother Charles. That attempt also failed and Patrick, calling himself Dr Peter Wallace, settled in Utrecht with his family.

Increasingly short of money, he found exile difficult, and for the first time, Patrick became depressed. It was Grizel who kept the family going, doing housework and steadily pawning what jewellery and other possessions the family had: 'provisions in exchange for a bauble.'

Though they were short of money, and often food, Patrick's table was open to any needy countryman for three years until William of Orange sailed from Holland for Britain in 1688 to become King William. Patrick was at last successful, landing with William as a friend, counsellor and supporter.

He was soon Sheriff of Berwickshire and in 1696 became Lord Chancellor of Scotland, Earl of Marchmont and Lord of Polwarth, Redbraes and Greenlaw. He was an ardent promoter of the Union of Parliaments in 1707, the peak of his political career. Although removed from office as sheriff in 1710 when the Tories came to power, Patrick, 'the most ardent Whig in Scotland', was reinstated in 1715.

Age gradually caught up with the man who had been through so much, and he spent his final years as a widower in Berwick-upon-Tweed. But his spirit was undaunted; and during a final visit by the equally heroic Grizel, now married to the son of Patrick's unfortunate friend Baillie of Jerviswoode, he insisted on being carried into the hall on a chair as family and friends danced.

"See, Grizel!" he said. "Though your father can't dance, he can still beat time with his foot!"

He died in Berwick on 1 August 1724, in his 83rd year, an example of piety, courage and patriotism, as was his splendid daughter.

Retold by Fordyce Maxwell

The late 1600s were a dangerous time in Scotland, particularly if you were a man of independent thought and principles. Both Charles I and Charles II, though from the Stuart royal family that had first united the crowns of Scotland and England, did much to alienate and antagonise the nation of their origin. Charles I, an avowed Catholic, sowed the seeds of the English Civil War in Scotland with his unpopular religious edicts. These did not sit well with a population that was now of a Protestant inclination, following the influence of John Knox (a minister in Berwick for a while, before he returned to Edinburgh) and perhaps a general inclination towards independence of mind and action.

Those who resisted these religious dictates, while initially still wishing to remain loyal to the Crown, became known as Covenanters when they put their signature to the National Covenant in 1638, petitioning the King to think again.

Things quickly escalated, leading to the Civil War, Cromwell's Commonwealth and the eventual restoration of Charles II as King in 1660. He had an eye for revenge on the Scots in general and Covenanters in particular.

In 1663, the 'Killing Times' began in earnest. They lasted almost 30 years. Non-conforming ministers were expelled from their churches and the Scottish Church effectively went underground, or at least into secret meetings in isolated places. The King's troops became notorious for seeking out and killing anyone not conforming with their master's views, in vicious and bloody ways.

Many of Wilson's Tales tell of brutality and of heroic actions during this period. Peace of a kind eventually came in 1689, when the unpopular Stuarts' hold on the throne came to an end with the Glorious Revolution. James II was deposed, and the Protestant William of Orange came across the Channel to be crowned unopposed. Even so, Scotland's tribulations were to continue for another half-century or so, as many Scots rallied round the Jacobite cause.

Sir Patrick Hume, a Tale of the House of Marchmont was one of Wilson's own Tales and no doubt the story was well known to him. Like many of the Tales, it sounds almost too far-fetched to be true but is essentially factual and well documented.

What brought the authorities bearing down on Polworth to apprehend Hume was his involvement in the Rye House Plot, a plan to ambush the King and his brother James at Rye House as they returned to London from the horse races at Newmarket. The threat to his life was very real and present. The conspirators included George Baillie, a good friend of Hume's who was caught and executed, though his son survived and went onto marry Hume's daughter, Grizel. Another was Sir John Cochrane, who was also rescued by his daughter (another Grizel) and the subject of another Wilsons's Tale, *Grizel Cochrane: a Tale of Tweedmouth Muir.*

The King had a fortunate escape: a major fire at Newmarket caused his party to return home a day early, and the ambush never took place. The plot involved too many cooks for its own good, and it was quickly exposed and unwound.

The value of Hume's contribution seems debatable. Gilbert Burnet, a chronicler of the time, describes him as "a hot and eager man, full of passion and resentment and instead of minding the business then in hand he was always forming schemes… in which he was so earnest that he fell into perpetual disputes and quarrels". A second source refers to him as "a man incapable alike of leading and of following: conceited, captious and wrong-headed, an endless talker, a sluggard in action and active only against his own allies".

However, wanted he was. His hiding place in the dark family vaults can still be seen behind metal bars beneath Polworth Church, with stone coffins of ancestors the only company. It is no wonder soldiers would not think or fancy to search such a spooky place. The church is well worth a visit, and plaques commemorate the actions of those involved.

The family's adventures, particularly while in exile in Holland, were recorded and published by Sir Patrick Hume's grand-daughter, Lady Grisell Baillie Murray. Family letters in this publication detail their deteriorating finances. However, they returned with a triumphant and grateful William of Orange who, as William II, restored their estates and positions with the additional title of Earl of Marchmont.

The descendants of Hume and Grizel still live in the Borders. The titles and estates continued to be built-up through marriage, and senior bloodlines still occupy grand houses such as Mellerstain. The name Grizel has also continued in other branches of the family. Today, Grizel Kennedy, Sir Patrick's great (x7) grand-daughter, still has a napkin embroidered by the original Grizel Hume. However, this is not the one used to smuggle the sheep's head, unless she had the foresight as a teenager to know she would marry Sir George Baillie, whose name is found at the other end!

In latter compilations of the Tales, and other retellings of the story, it is Grizel who becomes the hero of the narrative as the Victorians became partial to female heroes such as Grace Darling and Florence Nightingale.

Background by Andrew Ayre

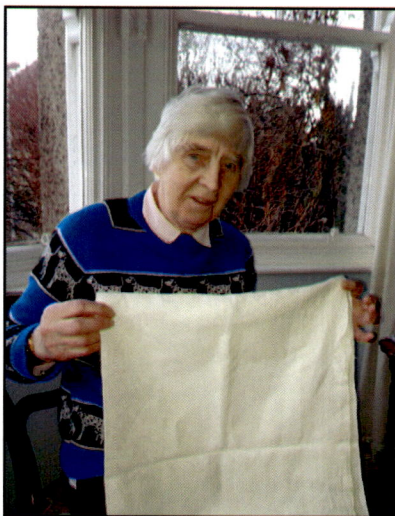

Grizel Kennedy, Sir Patrick Hume's great (x7) grand-daughter, holds a napkin embroidered by the original Grizel Hume. It includes the name of Grizel's husband, Sir George Baillie, whose father was executed.

Judith the Egyptian
or The Fate of the Heir of Riccon

It was a long time ago – as far ago as King Harry and his daughter Queen Elizabeth – that the first people of the Egyptians came to this land. Whether they really came from the land of the Pharaohs or if they were refugees from the land of Hindustan is way, way back in the mists of time and mystery.

But what I can tell you is this: round about that time, when the wanderers came north to this place, they began to make their winter residence around the areas of Spittal and Horncliffe and Rothbury – and particularly at Kirk Yetholm, which even to this day its known as the royal seat of the King of the Faa, the King of the Gypsies.

Way back maybe 300 or more years ago, there was a big man among the Gypsy folk of the Borders and he was called Lussha Fleckie. Now Lussha Fleckie was not just big in stature; he also was great. He was a champion at all of the sports that he excelled at and all things that he did he was champion of. He was an important man among the Border Gypsies. And as for his work, well: one day he would be a tinsmith and the next day perhaps a knife-grinder and maybe on the third day he would be a wandering piper, as the mood took him.

Lussha and his wife Mariam had an exquisite daughter called Judith. Judith was elegant, tall, graceful. She had a beautiful face with a dark, sultry complexion. And she had eyes the shapes of almonds and as black as the sloes, twinkling and lustrous. She was beautiful and she was vain, and her parents fed that vanity by decking her out with golden rings and trinkets from Lussha's silver urn.

This urn had been passed down to Lussha from his father and his father before him. It held their treasure and now it held Lussha's treasure, which he loved to bedeck his beautiful daughter with. In fact, she was known in all the land around as the Beautiful Gypsy.

From the very earliest days her mother, Mariam, had taught her the arts of fortune telling and palmistry. She excelled at this, so that all the noble, proud and wealthy ladies of Northumbria and Roxburghshire would be eager to have her come to tell their fortunes – for with her searching eyes she could make them tremble with joy or with trepidation as she wished. She was a favourite amongst them, yet they loved and feared her; and wherever she went she was decked in the cast-offs of their own finery.

It was early on in the year and a young sun came up over the Eildon Hills, when about 40 of the people of the Faa came there to make their camp. In no time at all they had set up their tents, they had raised up flaming bonfires underneath their cauldrons, and the smells of a savoury feast were blowing up into the air.

And when they had all eaten their fill and the brandy cup had gone round, Lussha Fleckie got up, he put on his pipes and started to play. All the people – men, women and children – jumped up and started to dance to the merry reels. There in the very middle of all of them swung Judith the Beautiful Gypsy, with her long tresses waving out behind her like the queen of the dance that she was, and her partner was a young lad of about 20; his name was Gemmel Graham.

Now, Gemmel Graham was the most agile, the most daring, the strongest, the fastest and the fiercest of all his race, proud and passionate. In fact, he was very like Lussha Fleckie had been himself when he was a younger man, and he was often Judith's partner at the dance. As they swung round, all the people were filled with merriment.

Judith and Gemmel had known each other all their lives. Judith had seen Gemmel in the Tweed right up to his neck, wrestling with a salmon and throwing it out with his bare hands onto the side. She had seen him winning at every wrestling match and every sport; whilst he had seen Judith as she grew up, his passion grew and she was indeed the apple of his eye. But he was a jealous man, and he did not like any other person to look at her.

As they were dancing, over the hill came young Walter, the heir of Riccon.

He came over with his grey goshawk on his arm and his hound at his feet and his servant. They made their way over to where the music was playing, and as they arrived Walter looked down and was dazzled by Judith's beauty.

Gemmel saw him, and saw his look. When the dance was over he led Judith back to her father, who was sitting on the green bank, and then strode straight up to the young laird. He put his chin forward into Walter's face and said: "What do you want, sir? And what is it that you are looking at?"

"Ha!" said the young man on the horse. "I am looking at your partner, for she is the prettiest girl that I have ever seen and I intend to talk with her."

"Sir," said Gemmel, "you are not welcome here. You have your horse and your hound, you have your servant. I don't covet what you have, don't you covet what I have! Go away from here – you are not invited and you are not welcome. I, Gemmel Graham, am warning you."

Now Walter wasn't about to be threatened by anybody. He turned his horse and said: "Tut! I am not frightened by you! I shall talk to her." He put his spur into his horse – but just as he did so, Gemmel grabbed the reins and pulled it down. Horse and man fell to the floor, and straight away Gemmel was on top of Walter.

Lussha jumped up. "Gemmel get off, get off that man!" he said. "What kind of a welcome is that? Judith, bring that gentleman over here. Gemmel, get off that man, you tyke!"

So Judith went over and Gemmel took his hand from young Walter's throat. He threw himself down on the grass, muttering bitterly to himself, with a great scowl like a thundercloud sitting on his brow. Judith did what she'd been told and led the young laird over to where Lussha was sitting. He hadn't been sitting there very long nor talking to Lussha for very long before letting him know how very delighted he was with the looks of his daughter. Well, Lussha smiled and Miriam looked triumphant, and when Lussha got up with his pipes to play for the next dance, it wasn't Gemmel Graham that was her partner, it was young Walter, the heir of Riccon.

Gemmel looked and he saw and he ground his teeth. At the end of the dance Walter took a costly ring from his finger and put it onto Judith's finger, and he whispered, "Wear this for my sake". Gemmel leapt up, but too late – for Walter was already on his horse, galloping away back home.

Most of the elders knew that the young Laird of Riccon would be drinking from a poisoned chalice if he stayed looking for Judith. So they decided by majority to cease their fun and feasting, break up the camp and set off away from that place. They knew from both Lussha Fleckie's temperament and that of young Gemmel that, because of this slight on Gemmel, there could be blood between them and it could mean a deadly fight.

So the tents were taken down. And all the while, as the camp was being broken up, Gemmel stood there with his back to a tree trunk, his hands across his chest, stamping the ground and whistling to himself and staring with a scowl like a horseshoe at Lussha's tent.

Well, the very next morning, Walter's servant came to him and told him that Judith and her family had moved away to camp near Kelso. That same night, Walter rode down to where they had camped because already he had determined that she would become Lady of Riccon Hall. When he got there the sun was setting, and in its gleams he saw Judith on her own – looking at the ring he had given her, turning her hand, seeing it glinting in the setting sun. He rode up, dismounted and threw himself on his knees, took her hand in his and said: "Beautiful lady of my dreams!"

It was a rhapsody of love. Judith was very, very impressed! When Gemmel had said loving words to her, it was always about how wonderful his own exploits were – boasts about who he had just wrestled to the ground and how much he had just hunted. But Walter, he talked all about Judith, how beautiful she was, how graceful she was, how sweet she was and how much like a treasure she was to him! These words fired her vanity; and even as he was on his knees in front of her she could see herself, all jewelled, as the Lady of Riccon Hall.

By the time he left they had arranged to meet again – and indeed they met again a number of times. He wooed her very well, and every time he did, he bought her a trinket. He saw how well the first, that ring, had gone down with Judith, and the next time he came he gave her a golden watch that he had got in Geneva, that hung on a golden chain. He took it off his neck and put it on hers – where she felt the ticking of her own heart, even faster and louder than the watch.

Both Mariam and Lussha knew they were meeting. They saw Judith was getting jewels and gold and silver from this young man and yet they did nothing, said nothing. The year rolled on, more and more meetings were had, and the family eventually decided that they would spend some time in an old ruin down by Twizel Bridge.

Young Walter had been invited in to eat with them, and they had just sat down to a fine meal when in rushed a hound. Judith recognised it straight away.

"Oh!" she said. "This is Gemmel's hound. You must get up now and flee, for if he finds you here he will kill you."

"I am not fleeing from any man," said Walter. "I am not scared, let the braggart come!"

"No, no," said Lussha. "You must go. You don't know him like we know him. If you stay here and he comes there will be dead bodies and blood in this room, for he has a fearsome temper. You must go." And between them they shoved the man out of the door and down the banks of the Tweed.

Moments afterwards, Gemmel stalked in. He looked at the food on the ground and he looked at them and he scowled.

"Well, welcome Gemmel," said Mariam. "We've not seen you for a long time. Sit down and have something to eat with us, we have plenty."

"So I see," he said. "Were you expecting somebody? I dare say this food wouldn't be fine enough for his palate."

"What do you mean?" said Lussha. "What are you saying to me?"

"You know very well what I am saying to you," he said.

"Well," Lussha retorted, "if you have something that you want to say, say it."

"Aye I do. But I will say it to Judith." He looked over at Judith and she had shrunk away into a dark corner – her hands over the watch so that he wouldn't see it, not thinking of the gold chain that glittered in the firelight.

"Would you come with me, Judith?" said Gemmel. "I need to speak to you." She looked timidly over at her father. Lussha muttered, "Well, Gemmel, I don't know. Your blood's up – you might harm her."

"Harm her?" said Gemmel. "Harm her? I'll give you my thumb I'll not harm her. Will you come, Judith?"

She got up, and with her father's permission she went out with Gemmel. They went a little way along to an old tree and stood there in silence for a while. Eventually, Gemmel said: "Where did you get all those ornaments, Judith? Was it out of your father's silver pot?"

She said nothing, but she trembled. "Oh, Judith," he said. "I see what it is now, Judith. Do you not remember all the times that we sat beneath a hawthorn and told each other how much we loved each other and I told you that you were dearer to me than the golden star in the sky?"

She said nothing, but she trembled again and wept. "Do you not remember your vows, Judith?" he asked. "The vows that you gave me, false Judith?"

"Let me go, I must go!" she said as she struggled and wriggled and tried to get away.

"Then go!" he said. "But don't come back to me – and beware the next time we meet."

The year went on a little more. One beautiful evening, as a harvest moon rose up over golden fields of corn, underneath the birches and down by the Tweed near Norham Castle stood Walter and Judith.

Walter was asking her if she would go to live with him as lady of his castle.

"Oh, Walter," she said, "I don't know! You say you love me, but you might not love me so well if you have me at your castle."

"How could you say that?" said Walter. "You know that I love you."

"Well," she said, "I don't know your ways so well. Maybe if you would come and tell my father and my mother and all my people that I am to be your own true wife and the Lady of Riccon Hall… then maybe I'll come with you."

"Oh no you won't!" A great voice burst from the wood – and immediately there was the loud crack of a pistol and Walter dropped dead at her feet. Judith's screams were so loud that they made all the birds rise in the trees and she dropped to her knees beside her lover on the ground.

Above her loomed Gemmel . "Yes, kiss the lips of your bonny bridegroom!" he spat. "Kiss them away, and kiss that spirit as it leaves his body. For he'll not have you now, and I don't want you any more. Farewell, false, false Judith!" And he threw down the pistol and ran shouting and roaring into the woods.

"There was a loud crack of a pistol and Walter dropped dead at her feet."
An original illustration from Wilson's Tales of the Borders

Judith wept, her tears fell on Walter's face. And when her people finally found her, she was lying with her arms around the neck of a dead man. Her father picked her up and tried to carry her away; but she wailed and screamed.

"Gemmel! It was wicked, wicked Gemmel killed him! But no – no, it was me! It was false Judith killed him!" And as she was taken away she screamed and wailed piteously. They found the pistol – but never the murderer, though they looked long and hard.

Another year went by. This time down by Norham Castle there was a young woman, a beautiful young woman dressed as a Gypsy. She had a child at her breast and, though the Tweed was full, she tried to cross the river. As she did, an angry flood came up and swept them away. The woman was rescued, but the baby was never seen again.

Years went by again, 10, 20, 30. Still every year a woman came, a woman drained of beauty, the colour gone from her hair just as grief had drained the senses from her mind. And as she came to the Tweed, to that fatal spot, she crooned to her lost child, "Come back, my bonny child! You are the true heir of Riccon and I the true Lady of Riccon Hall. It was Gemmel killed your bonny daddy… wicked Gemmel killed your daddy – not me, 'twas not me!"

That was a cold and bitter winter, the winter that they found the body of the old Gypsy frozen underneath her red cloak. They took the corpse and buried it under the shadow of Norham Castle.

And not so very long afterwards an old man, an old sailor, came to live in that district. And again, not so very long afterwards, he was on his deathbed. He left a cap full of golden rings and silver rings, and a dying wish that he would be buried next to Judith who had been the Beautiful Gypsy – and that his initials, GG, would be carved on the stone that was set above them, and so it was done.

And that is the end of this tale. However, Judith is still remembered in the lyrics of the Border Ballad, *Judith the Egyptian*.

> *"The black-eyed Judith, fair and tall*
> *Attracted the heir of Riccon Hall.*
> *For years and years was Judith known*
> *Queen of a wild world all her own –*
> *By Wooler Haugh, by River Till*
> *By Coldstream Bridge and Flodden Hill –*
> *Until, at length, one morn when sleet*
> *Hung frozen round the traveller's feet,*
> *By a grey rain on Tweedside*
> *The creature laid her down and died."*

Retold by Mary Kenny

Judith the Egyptian
Background

The original Tale, with its catalogue of error and prejudice, is not one of Wilson's better stories. Mary Kenny is to be congratulated for producing such an excellent modern version, which is not only acceptable to the 21st century but is eminently more readable than the original.

I can find no historical basis for the Tale. Its alternative title, *The Fate of the Heir of Riccon*, seems designed to convey some geographical connection to a historical event; but I can find no place name in the Borders, Northumberland or anywhere in Scotland that corresponds to Riccon.

The 'Border Ballad' quoted in the Tale is not to be found in any compilation or minstrelsy of these traditional verses. The lines lack the tautness and economy of word so typical of the true ballads. I suspect it is from Wilson's own pen, as it shares some similarities with his *The Tweed near Berwick*. The easiest test is to remember that the ballads were originally sung to the accompaniment of a harp or other single instrument. Try to sing this 'Border Ballad': it doesn't work.

Wilson's original Tale begins with a lengthy preamble about the origins of the Roma or Gypsy peoples. This contains some details that are now accepted as fact about their origins in Northwest India, not in Egypt, as had been commonly thought, but also much prejudice and error. It is, I suppose, typical of the 19th-century European view of 'lesser' peoples. It is noteworthy that Wilson (though not Mary Kenny's retelling) also mentions the Jews, who suffered similar racist bias.

The Roma peoples were originally welcomed into 15th-century Scotland in the reign of James IV. They acted as dancers and minstrels, often appearing at court. James wrote to the King of Denmark in his own hand, describing Anthony Gavin, the leader of the gypsies, as 'Earl Anthony of Little Egypt'.

James V continued in this vein, granting Johnnie Faa his protection and giving him the right to administer justice to the Gypsy people, describing him as 'owre louvit Johnnie Faa, the Lord and Earl of

Little Egypt'. This title and right was extended to Faa's son and heir, John Warren, in 1540.

Unfortunately for the Roma peoples, James VI was not similarly disposed. Bigoted, paranoid and devoid of interest in any culture he did not see as fit, he was intent on the suppression of all views other than his own. Anyone likely to show independence of thought or deed was suspect.

His arrogant espousal of the doctrine of the Divine Right of Kings, which he passed to his son, was eventually to cause the Civil War and the execution of Charles I.

Before that, this malignant monarch was responsible for the deaths of many a poor woman deemed to be a witch, for initiating the slow decline of the Gaelic culture in Scotland, and for the persecution of the Gypsies. He described them as 'sorcerers, vagabonds and common thieves', and in 1609 they were banished from Scotland under pain of death.

Many of the Faas were indeed hanged. Women and children were indicted and sentenced 'to be taken to some convenient pairt and drowned till deed'. The fact that some of the latter were reprieved on condition that they left the country does not mitigate the savagery of the King's law.

Thereafter, the Gypsies were forced into a nomadic life in the hills and countryside, always trying to stay one jump ahead of the law. This may well be the source of the continuing prejudice shown to Judith's people up until the time of Wilson's Tale.

This attitude of the superiority of the white and, particularly, the Anglo-Saxon race persisted into the 20th century. It can be found in Dickens, Conan Doyle, Buchan, 'Sapper' and many other writers, as well as the caricatured portrayals of other peoples in films up until the 20th century.

Similarly, casual prejudice against Jews and Gypsies was commonplace in literature at the time of *Wilson's Tales*.

John Hoyland (1750–1831), an English Quaker and author who lived in Yorkshire and the Midlands, published *A Historical Survey of the Customs, Habits and Present State of the Gypsies* in 1816. Wilson may well have been introduced to this book by his friend James Everett (1784–1872): it's reasonable to suppose that Everett, as a Methodist preacher who also lived and worked in Yorkshire and the Midlands, either knew Hoyland or was at least aware of his work.

Hoyland's book contains much about the Gypsies' supposed predilection for eating animals that have died of disease, which Wilson refers to more than once in his Tale (again, omitted in Mary Kenny's retelling). This material is not found in any other references to Roma cuisine. Eating such meat would appear to have occurred only in circumstances of dire poverty: perhaps the reference to 'creatures killed by God's hand' (a phrase Wilson gives to Judith's father, Lussha) was simply a device by the Gypsy peoples Hoyland encountered, to maintain their pride despite their reduced circumstances.

In Judith, it is unlikely that Lussha Fleckie, being a fairly wealthy man, would have needed to dine in such a manner, though Wilson again displays his prejudices in his description of the man as 'idle' and 'a vagrant' when Lussha describes himself as 'free'.

Even in his description of the beautiful Judith, he cavils at her complexion: "tinged with the tawny hue of her race".

The Tale itself is a fairly simple one. Judith, the beautiful girl with an obsessive suitor, Gemmel Graeme, rejects him for another of perceived higher station. The new lover, the Laird of Riccon, is killed by Graeme, who flees the country. Judith is driven mad by grief and wanders the country with her newborn child, the heir to Riccon. She is nearly drowned while trying to ford the Tweed at Ladykirk, and the child is lost in the flood waters.

A curious coincidence is that James IV nearly drowned while crossing the Tweed, and had Ladykirk Parish Church erected in 1503 to celebrate his survival.

Judith loses her mind completely and, for 30 years, haunts the spot of the infant's death. Finally, she is found frozen to death near Norham Castle. Later, Gemmel Graeme returns from foreign wars where he had sought refuge after murdering the Laird of Riccon. He asks to be buried beside her.

There are some familiar Border Ballad themes in Wilson's Tale: possessive love, murder of suitors, grief-stricken lovers, infant deaths. But the Tale lacks the impact of the balladeers' sparse verses. It's hard for the reader to get emotionally involved with the fate of characters who are two-dimensional and lacking in depth.

Judging by Wilson's preamble, it seems he got hold of some information first and then wrote a Tale around it. Information about characters and situations should emerge from a story, rather than being presented as a block of introductory narration as it is here.

I suspect that Wilson had read Hoyland's book, possibly getting it from Everett, and used much of the spurious material contained therein to give a simple story a gloss of exoticism by making the heroine a Gypsy.

He committed the ultimate journalistic error in not checking the sources, the Gypsy people themselves. Thus he reinforced existing misconceptions and prejudices which could have been avoided. Had he done some background research he could have produced a Tale with more original colour and background. There is no doubt he was under pressure to write to meet the demand for copy, but, in this case, he falls short.

Background by Dr Michael Fenty

Kate Kennedy

Many years ago, the great grey castle of Innerkepple remained as a staunch survivor of the constant tug of war between England and Scotland. Its rugged walls were pitted with battle scars from the engines of war, scars remembered by name in the stories of old.

The master of this relic, Walter Kennedy, or Innerkepple, as he was commonly known, resembled his old stone keep. He was a rough and burly old baron but, like the Tokay wine of which he was so fond, he had softened and mellowed with the passing of time. In truth, the old greybeard's deep friendship with the grape only increased the good humour and joviality of the man as his years advanced. Snug in his old wainscoted hall, contentedly imbibing spiced Tokay from a goblet gifted to his forebear by King James I, the Baron's thoughts generally revolved around three choice subjects: his castle, his wine and his family tree.

If Walter was a stout old limb of the ancestral tree of Innerkepple, his daughter Kate Kennedy was a strong young twig full of the green. Kate was bold, beautiful and buxom. She fairly sparkled with good health and young blood, and her nature was as merry as her father's when he was in his cups.

As to the wine, well, this was a time-consuming subject, for to a connoisseur like himself each and every year of its existence was a triumph deserving of a song. The best song of all to the Baron's ear was sung to the air *The Guidwife of Tullybody* and detailed the swashbuckling deeds of the Barons of Innerkepple and their noble castle. The painted faces of these same warriors loomed down from the walls of the hall.

Now Kate had certainly inherited her father's good humour and she cared little for high breeding. If she wanted to laugh or shout, she did so with alacrity, for there was no room for moping or melancholy in Kate's life. Nor did she have room for the cobwebs of history in which her father wrapped himself. She heard with cool disdain his reverence for the grey turrets of his old strength, and praises for the ancestors who fell in glory at Homildon and Flodden. Kate Kennedy preferred life, this very day! Top of her list for a lover was youth and beauty, not the careless flaunting of life on the battlefield.

However, if Innerkepple was merry, his neighbour most certainly was not.

Otterstone, named after his own castle, was an old and bitter foe. That there should be strife between them was no great surprise, since the Borderland had been full of rough-feuding families since ancient times. Their abrasive habits were fuelled through the reigns of Henry VIII and James V, who added religious aggressions to the chaos.

This sour neighbour, Magnus Fotheringham, had long been embroiled in a grim feud with Kenneth, Innerkepple's father, and nursed a deadly spite in his heart towards the whole house. The merry Baron had twice defended himself, with the help of his loyal and adoring retainers, and repulsed his splenetic aggressor with slaughter on both sides.

Despite all this and in vain, Innerkepple had persisted in attempting to bury the hatchet and offer the hand of friendship over a smoking flagon of spiced wine.

Then, one fine day, when he was out riding the marches with 10 of his men, he was ambushed by Otterstone and 20 men. Innerkepple's guard rallied around their chief and fought like lions, while their master shouted to his enemy to hold: "Otterstone, man! Stop the fecht! A pint of my auld canary will be better poured out between us than the bluid of our men spilt! I want no feud, and I'm no' answerable for the wrangs o' ma faither! I would sooner the blood of our houses be mixed at the Haley Kirk, man! I will gie ye the hand of my dochter Kate for your son to wed!"

But his parley was drowned by the roars of his men, from the heat of battle and from indignation at the suggestion of such an unthinkable match, for they dearly loved their kind and cheerful mistress. Otterstone mistook his muffled yells as battle cries, especially as Innerkepple waved the white handkerchief he'd just used to staunch the blood of one of his wounded men.

The bloodstained cloth looked to all, on both sides, more like a signal of revenge than the intended sign of peace.

It was at this point that an extraordinary vision appeared. Out from the castle galloped a detachment, and at their head was Kate Kennedy, in helmet and armour and wielding a sword above her head. The voices and spirits of Innerkepple's defenders ascended to new heights, and while the good Baron continued to yell peace to his splenetic enemy, Kate rallied her troops with triumphant looks and commands. Meanwhile, Otterstone harried his troops to fight for their skins, reputations and honour from the unutterable horror of defeat at the hands of a mere girl. And oh, what a girl!

"Press on, brave vassals of Innerkepple!" cried Kate with a flashing smile to her adoring army. "He that kills the most of Otterstone's men will win a kiss from Kate Kennedy! And if that's not enough to make you fight like lions you should be hung by chains from the towers of Otterstone!"

As she spoke she whirled her light sword around her head, wounding any who came within reach of her father. He was aghast at this bloodthirsty side previously unknown in his darling girl, the same daughter whose hand he had just proffered as a peace offering!

"By the bones of Camilla!" she laughed between slashes. "And I thought I was only fit for sewing battle scenes on satin, and laughing as I killed a knight with my needle! But I have Innerkepple in my veins after all! Ha! Just one glance of my eye has more power to command than the proudest baron in all the Borders!"

Spurred on by the electrifying inspiration of their mistress, Innerkepple's men soon had the upper hand, while Otterstone's broke ranks and fled. They would all have been cut down in flight if Kate had not called back her troops in mercy.

Glowing in triumph, Kate seemed to her father to have grown. Normally she would kill her suitors with her looks, torment them with her wits, and bewitch them with her restless spirit. But now... he decided he must have her portrait made to hang in his wainscoted hall along with Lewie of Homildon and Watt of Flodden.

Later on, in that same hall, father and daughter raised a goblet of Tokay together. "Grant rest to the souls I have slain," said she.

"What! Did ye kill ony of Otterstone's men?" he gasped.

"Every time I raised my visor," she replied.

"Oh, ye wicked imp!" chuckled Innerkepple, as they went to tend the wounded and raise cups to victory. Those cups were raised many times into the night.

Otterstone, meanwhile, was full of bile and black spirits, nursing wounds of shame at his ignominious defeat and loss of men, and at the hands of his enemy's daughter! He sent for his son, who had lived in France since childhood...

Time passed quietly enough. Innerkepple's love of wine deepened and his reputation as the most jovial baron in the Borders was cemented. Kate's fame also increased, though she was regarded an enigma. Suitors were dazzled by her many charms yet continued to be dashed by her cleverness and cruelly devilish wiles. The Baron quietly kept a wish for peace and friendship in his heart, and Kate also, despite her recent diversion, wished for the same.

Now King James was gathering men from the country and a detachment was drafted from Innerkepple. Though at Kate's insistence they were billeted at no greater distance than 10 miles, still this left the castle with scant defence. Inside the wainscoted hall the Tokay flowed while Kate continued to invent new ways to kill her embroidered knights.

Then one fine day a wine merchant arrived with his mules and panniers to barter with the good Baron, who welcomed him to the hall with gusto. From her window seat, Kate saw and heard the drawbridge lowered, the stranger enter with his beasts, and then one of her men signalling to her, so she descended carefully to courtyard to investigate.

When she strolled nonchalantly into the hall shortly afterwards, she found her father and the merchant sitting at the table supping and sampling from a large wine vessel. The Baron was both delighted and inspired by his guest and his wares. The quality and rarity of the wine was as pleasing as the flattering conversation of the young Frenchman.

"Now, have ye ony more of this treasure, man?" he said, smacking his lips over the goblet. "I thought I was the only one in Scotland with any of the '90 vintage. It is rarer than gold!"

"Ah may wee, noble sir, I have just five barrels in my celliers at Berwick," he answered with a smile.

"Well, I could walk on my bare feet to Berwick just to see and taste it," chuckled the Baron. "But, Kate, what is that clattering in the courtyard?"

A nervous shadow passed over the Frenchman's face.

"Oh monsieur, it is nothing," said Kate. "I have just sent a man to Selkirk to get my sandals mended and he has set off with unnecessary speed."

This answer satisfied both men, who returned to the important matter in hand: namely, the price.

While gazing carelessly from the window, Kate watched the merchant from the corner of her eye. She suspected a plot from Otterstone, but could see no grain of familiarity or of similarity to the old chief. No indeed: this young Frenchman was intriguing, very well made and pleasingly handsome, and in a few short minutes she set her designs on him. Wisely she calculated that, with all her unique qualities, when her match was made it must be by her own hand.

However, when a price was finally settled for the wine and with the bonus of carousal for the retainers thrown in, Kate saw treachery in her lovely French merchant. She ambled nonchalantly out of the hall and then raced down the steps to give orders to her men. Soon the merchant appeared in the courtyard, opening a large vessel of wine for the willing retainers, and soon the sounds of cheers and revelling travelled back up to Innerkepple's hall. Little did the Frenchman know that Kate had replaced the strong liquor with a thin and watery variety, and that the hilarity below was really a joke at his own expense.

In the great hall, conversation between Baron and merchant turned to the wish for peace with his neighbour on the Baron's part, talk of a mysterious son, and his courageous daughter Kate's recent victory. Watching from the window, she saw a sign she had been seeking and drifted silently out of the hall. Under cover of raucous drunken singing, her men learned the next steps of her plan; and as darkness closed in, so revelry faded to the rumbling, oblivious silence of sleep.

The Baron's seneschal staggered into the cosy chamber, and in lugubriously outraged tones declared that he was the only man standing in the castle who wasn't stone drunk! As proof, the ringing snores of the men below competed with the screeches of owls in the turrets. Kate yawned, stretched and retired for the night, behind the curtain, while a grumbling Innerkepple and apologetic merchant sat down to supper before another course of Tokay.

"Harrumph! Huh! That's a grand chorus in the courtyard, monsieur," muttered the Baron. "Singing, snoring and groaning are the three successive acts of the wassailers! They would have been better getting their supper!"

"Hellas, you prick my memory, mon noble Innerkepple! My poor mules! Cruel master that I am to forget their souper! Pardon me, mon cher Baron; I must give them one leetle feed from my panniers."

Kate, peeking from behind the curtain, had noticed how her father grew sleepy, while the charming merchant grew twitchy. Like a shadow she followed as he crept from the hall, descended, and then crossed the body-strewn courtyard. Suddenly, fleet as a deer, he sprang upon the parapet and produced a strange blue phosphorescent light, which he held aloft and swung purposefully from side to side. Outside the walls a shrill bugle sounded, and the merchant swung into action to lower the drawbridge. As it thudded to earth the tramp, tramp, tramp of marching invaders filled the night.

Then, like an onrushing flood, a dark, dense body of men rushed from the fir woods, pressing in behind the invaders. At the same instant, the drunken retainers within leapt to their feet, rushed forward brandishing their weapons, and so trapped the invaders both front and rear. "Caught in our own snare!" growled old Otterstone, immediately comprehending his helpless position.

"Disarm them, men!" The shrill command came from Kate Kennedy.

The scuffle was short and sharp. Innerkepple's retainers had been secretly recalled from royal duty, and the seemingly debauched men were soon taking arms from Otterstone's men like toys from children, such was their surprise and dismay. Every single eye turned to the woman who stood sword in one hand, flaming brand in the other as the genius of their misfortune!

Soon all were gathered tightly inside the wainscoted hall, where the sleeping Baron had woken, astonished and disconcerted, to find his bitter rival Otterstone beside him.

"Right glad I am," said Kate with determination, "to meet under the auspices of friendship in my father's hall! Father, I offer you the hand of Otterstone. Otterstone, I offer you the hand of Innerkepple.

"Born nobles and neighbours!" she chided "Educated and civilised men! Baptised Christians, why should ye be foes? But above all, why should one strike with the sword the hand that holds the cup of friendship?"

"What is this?" Innerkepple stammered in amazement. "Am I dreaming, or a prisoner in my ain castle? Am I betrayed, and where is the wine merchant? And as to friendship,", turning to his foe, "is it possible that you have repented your ill will and come to make amends, Otterstone?"

Kate looked foursquare in their enemy's face. "So," she said, "will you still refuse the hand of peace?"

Otterstone hesitated, sighed deeply, and then, as if clouds dropped from his eyes and the sun began to shine, he smiled. Stepping forward, he took Innerkepple by the hand and shook it heartily and long, to the murmured approval of the whole hall.

"Now," said Kate, "we must seal it with a toast. Where is that wine merchant?"

The young fellow was brought in along with the hampers of wine, and in considerable surprise stood amidst the company, looking at Innerkepple, the majestic Kate, and not least the smile on the face of his father, for of course he was young Otterstone!

"Hector, lad, the game is up: this maiden has outwitted us. So, off with your disguise man, and show your true colours!"

Hector gladly threw off his wig and the clumsy clothes which covered his armour. Now truly, there stood a young man of the most exquisite beauty!

"Hector Fotheringham, the wine merchant!" cried the Baron brightly. "Well, well! Is this the way you bring your lovers to Innerkepple, Kate? And in the safest of disguises, too, you baggage? As for you, Hector, I need no bribe of Tokay, for you are a fine youth and I see you are made for my dochter Kate!"

"Aye, and your dochter made for him, too!" laughed Otterstone.

Cheers rang out from masters and men, and pealed through the halls and turrets of Innerkepple. The wine that had been intended for treachery was now circulated freely and opened the hearts of all the company, and many's the joyful toast was made that night with the Tokay.

And so, dear reader, peace was restored at last. And in a very short time the venerable Houses of Innerkepple and Otterstone were united by the marriage of Hector Fotheringham and the unsurpassable Kate Kennedy!

Retold by Mary Kenny

Kate Kennedy
Illustrator's notes

John Mackay Wilson describes his *Tales of the Borders* as 'Historical, Traditionary and Imaginative'. The combination of these elements in each Tale varies, but before embarking on illustrating the story of Kate Kennedy I tried to separate fact from fiction. Although I'd be happy to be proved wrong, in my view this Tale is largely an imaginative representation of a typical 16th-century Borders feud, romanticised and fairly light-hearted. It would make a good comic opera – and to set the scene I'd rely on costume and an authentic sense of place.

Page 35: Kate and her jovial father, Walter. He appears to be regaling her with tales of Kennedy bravery in battle, while she indulges him with good-humoured attention over a goblet of wine. The late afternoon sun is going down behind two of the Eildon Hills.

Page 36: In this scene we are high up in the Cheviot Hills by a waterfall on the College Burn in Northumberland. Otterstone, mounted on a horse and with halberd in hand, has just ordered his men to fire upon Walter Kennedy's patrol, despite a good natured plea from old Walter to share some of his wine.

Page 38: This image of Kate leading her troops into battle is a piece of romanticised gothic. Kate's heroic pose on the back of her horse also has very intentional echoes of the equestrian statue of Joan of Arc by Paul Dubois.

Page 40: This representation of Innerkepple is an imaginative composite of several different Borders fortifications. The distant figure waving to the guards above the drawbridge is Otterstone's son, disguised as a French wine merchant and seeking revenge.

Page 41: The Baron in convivial conversation with the young 'wine merchant', whose samples he is consuming with enthusiasm. Otterstone's men are concealed in the trees outside the castle, ready to storm it once Innerkepple's men are too drunk to fight.

Page 43: Kate, sensing treachery, waters down the wine offered to the Baron's men by the wine merchant. She is haunted by a memory of Alexander the Great warning his troops not to drink from a poisoned stream.

Page 45: Outwitted by Kate's guile, Otterstone's troops are trapped on two sides attempting to cross the Baron's drawbridge.

Page 47: Having brought the two warring families together, Kate accepts Hector Fotheringham's hand in marriage amidst great celebration and carousing. Peace reigns at last!

Illustrations and notes by Charles Nasmyth

The Trials of the Rev Samuel Austin

The Reverend Samuel Austin was born around 1600 in Closeburn. His father was a shepherd on the farm of Auchincairn. The young Austin was home-educated by an uncle, a former soldier who had retired on a small government allowance. A man well educated for the time, he took special care that the young boy should benefit from his knowledge, learning and the strength to be had from a connection with God.

On summer evenings the pair would climb the mound of stones that gave the farm its name; and with the young lad ensconced upon this throne of stones and one step closer to the heavens, his uncle would turn his talk to that of the Reformation and the reformers. He would tell how during the efforts to build and support the Scottish Kirk, those 'prisoners of conscience' suffered torture, death and wrongdoing.

As his thoughts and body matured, young Samuel became daily attached to the cause of liberty and the Kirk (or as we might say, Presbytery). In due course, at his uncle's expense, he was formally educated for the Church and at the tender age of 20 was called unanimously to serve the neighbouring Parish of Penpont.

As time passed his great sponsor and friend, his uncle, died, followed soon afterwards by Samuel's parents. After this last bereavement his only sister, who was blind, came to live with him at the manse. He was duly accommodated into the Church, and the following entry appears in his diary: "16 September, 16--. This day I have been solemnly inducted into the pastoral charge of many souls. Lord, what am I or my father's house, that thou shouldst honour me thus!"

Some 12 months after his accommodation he married Elizabeth Shiels, and for some years it seems the Minister of Penpont enjoyed a good life.

Then his testing began.

Charles II was reinstated to his throne, due largely to the Scottish Presbyterians and the pragmatism of General Monk. And so it was, with a Stuart once more at the nation's helm, a man both infamous and treacherous, the betrayal of the Covenanters, some of the very people who enabled his restoration, began to gather pace and the 'Killing Times' commenced.

It was of no account to Charles that he had signed the National League and Covenant. Self-seeking and with no moral compass, he was swayed and manipulated by those whose counsel he chose to accept. The governance of the Christian Church on both sides of the border would now be carried out by the privileged. Clerics of high social rank and power, Fairful, Wishart, Sydserff, Mitchel and Leighton, to name but a few, were consecrated. They were sent to Scotland, titled bishops; James Sharp was made archbishop. All were to take their seats as an Estate in the Scottish Parliament. Here they would forbid all induction into Church offices unless under their authority.

The reaction was immediate: uproar and anger by both lay and clerical members throughout Scotland. Feelings ran highest throughout the counties south of the Forth and Clyde. It was seen as a throwing-over of all that their predecessors had vigorously fought to secure, at times to the death, for more than 150 years. Worse, ceding the power of the people back to the King and Church was considered a submission to an illegal and arbitrary adjustment of star chambers, secret courts and justice by connection.

In Scotland, religion was never a one-subject matter. Woven through it were questions of political freedom and equality under law. In 1662, Covenanters came to realise that compromise over one would make inevitable the surrender of the others.

And so it was that during this year, Austin's failure to seek his confirmation by the newly appointed Bishop of Galloway, within whose diocese Penpont sat, led to his being summonsed. He was ordered to appear before Bishop Hamilton to account for his wilful refusal to comply with the authorities.

As someone inducted and ordained according to the rules of the Presbyterian Church, he considered himself unable to obey the Bishop's mandate. This stance placed him and his family at risk, and in due course condemned his son.

His only son, William, a budding preacher himself, had scarlet fever, a recurring illness that had afflicted him for some time. While it had not yet succeeded in taking him away, it was daily making him weaker. In a bid to secure the best chance of his survival, the boy's mother pleaded with her husband to meet with the Bishop and do as was being asked of him.

Her husband, however, was not to be persuaded. His higher calling trumped even his love for his son. On a cold and frosty Saturday in January, while the hills were snow-capped and ponds and lakes turned to ice, the family gathered in prayer. As had become customary, the service was led by young William.

William always gave his all in his worship, and this morning he came to his prayers with all the zeal he could muster. It was while he was on his knees and so engaged that the door was rudely opened. A collective of coarse-bearded and heavily armed dragoons entered the room, led by one General Dalziell of Binns, the King's Commander in Chief, with direct orders to subdue the Covenanters.

"What have we here?" asked Dalziell, pushing the young preacher with his foot. "Why, here we have a whole batch: man, mistress, and maid…" Addressing the Reverend directly, he continued: "Enough of your chanting and grunting, you grey whiskered traitor! I have a message for you from his Majesty, God bless him and curse upon his enemies. The Lord Chancellor, at the behest of Lord Hamilton, Bishop of Galloway, has directed me to warn you that unless you accept ordination as an episcopal curate for his Lordship, following presentation before Queensberry, you must face the consequences."

"That," came the emphatic reply of the people's Presbyterian pastor, "will never happen. No force, earthly or otherwise, no threat of malice made by lord or bishop will ever effect such an outcome."

"In which damned case," spat back Dalziell, "you must all go now, the whole rag-tag rabble of you. Leave this snug, comfortable manse and go to that wide and roomy land of the northern county of Angus, far and away beyond the River Tay."

"Oh spare us!" came a hysterical shriek from Mrs Austin. Casting her dignity aside, she flung herself in supplication around the bearded monster's legs, hoping to give her pleas greater persuasion. She wailed most pitifully to be spared and in the same gasping breath promised her husband's compliance. Anything, so as to get these men to leave and allow the family to continue peacefully in the quiet enjoyment of their home.

The emotions that fired her petitions and the breathy, panicky voice only raised Dalziell's contempt, banishing even basic respect for a distressed human and replacing it with violent fury: "Get up, woman, and cease this pointless pleading! I know my duty."

Distressed and blinded by fear, the woman simply transferred her tactic to her husband. "Oh, Samuel Austin, look at me! Look in my face, whar ye said ye have often looked with pleasure. Look at your own Betty Sheils." But this test of his asserted love for her merely showed how little at this stage she appreciated the strength of his faith. Her outline of the cold and hardship that would face them if exiled fell upon a mindset as frozen and set as the ground beyond the manse doors.

Thoroughly bored by this spectacle, Dalziell could wait no more. "No more of your absurd ceremonies and false worship! Either listen to your wiser half and take promise to my master as is being asked of you or you shall leave this place immediately."

Although not persuaded from his path, Austin was touched by his wife's petitions. As his gaze fell upon his silent son he blurted out, the grief catching his words, "Willie, my son, what would you have me do?"

This religious child savant calmly regarded his father and spoke with a composure beyond his years: "Do your duty, leave the rest to God."

Humbled by his son's words, Austin turned and announced with renewed conviction: "We are ready, do your worst! I do not doubt that my God, who fed Elijah in the wilderness, will not permit the old, the blind, and my dying child to perish homeless and helpless. We shall go now to wherever the Lord decides."

Dalziell directed that the family be evicted in 24 hours. No place was to be left for them to shelter, so the Church and manse doors were to be locked on their departure. His contempt for their kind was encapsulated by his saying they should be unkenneled, rather than evicted.

The following Sunday was cold, clear and frosty, the ground dry and snow-free. A huge crowd of supporters had come. The Austin family with other local dignitaries were placed in a tent while the young Lord of Closeburn (who would soon pay the ultimate penalty for this exertion) sat behind the main speaker.

In his diary the Reverend reflected: "The Lord has been good and gracious this day. Five hundred Presbyterian believers partook of the bread of life. There was no hand to help, no voice to rouse but mine, and that of my poor dying child. His blessed spirit was indeed upon me in this great work; but my poor boy has laboured too hard in preaching and in prayer."

The next day saw the manse surrounded by carts, come to move the family's sticks of furniture and crockery to safe store until, if ever such time came, normality and they could return.

The weather was evil with storms. To attempt to journey in such conditions through the Lauder Hills would be sheer folly. But no one could harbour an outlaw without inviting their own downfall, so there was no alternative.

A kindly neighbour donated his cart upon which sat the aged, blind and sick, for all the world as if they were heading to the gallows. As the wheels began to turn, one mighty roar, a wail from all the parishioners, began to fill the air. And just as Christ was followed to, but could not be joined in Calvary, the family were followed; but here just as far as Thornhill.

That first night they spent in a public house. Young William was placed straight away in his bed, exhausted from his preaching and the anxiety brought on by his exile. He seemed beyond further movement despite the peril which not travelling would place them in. On the second day a military detachment came, with strict orders to convey Austin, dead or alive, to his destined place of banishment, beyond the Tay, to the ghetto containing all the other nonconformist ministers exiled from their parishes in the South.

The Reverend, sad beyond words, found little comfort even from his faith, so great was the pain of knowing he must leave his family and likely never see his son alive again. And for the boy, denied the blessing his father might give in his final hours of life, there was no salve.

At 10am the Reverend was frogmarched away by three of Dalziell's men. Though not untouched by the pathos of this separation, they were not deflected from fulfilling their military duty. And so they all marched slowly to Carron Bridge and Durrisdeer.

By Durrisdeer they paused for some refreshment, and in an uncharacteristic act of cunning the Reverend gave the men a large sum of money with which to drink his health. As this went on, he affected to join them and by his acting persuaded them that he was indeed 'this good fellow'. One of the soldiers refused to go further that night and threatened to shoot the first person who tried to dissuade him. Mid-flow in announcing his intent, drink robbed him of his senses and he abruptly collapsed into a chair in a drunken stupor.

The other two, though touched, remained resolute that they must march up to the Well Path to reach Ewland Foot that night. The Well Path is a narrow ravine which runs through the mountains separating Nithsdale from Clydesdale. The mountain walls are so steep that they meet the ravine floor at right angles. The pass is rough and winding, and when snow-clad is difficult to follow and fatally dangerous to miss.

In the dusky light of early evening they managed to get to the middle of the pass, where the drifting snow both checked them and obscured the true path. It settled on the edges of the path, extending it into an overhang of white icing that obscured the deadly hundred-foot drop beneath it.

Being acquainted with the pass, Austin had an advantage over his guards. He offered the men a swig from a bottle of brandy he had secured at the inn, and both men drew deeply from it to slake their thirsts. Pressing on to make up time, the men gave head to haste, neglecting care. For a short while their progress was swift, but in plunging forward they had not determined direction. Almost at once they fell through the mirage of path, clinging together as they went into the abyss.

At about four the following morning, some distance from this icy mishap, the boy's condition had worsened in the wake of his father's departure. The room was bathed in a low and soft light from a lamp placed by the bed. His mother sat by his head with a cup of cold water while his aunt massaged his now-swelling legs.

Without any indication of a recovery, William started to repeat prayers, psalms and texts with great clarity and beauty. Until, mid-sentence, he paused and, forcing himself up from his pillow, exclaimed: "My father, my father, my dear, persecuted father!"

Both mother and aunt imagined that he had begun to rave, and tried to press him down on his pillow. But then through the gloom the familiar voice of the preacher filled the room: "It is I indeed! Your earthly and real father, whom the Lord has delivered from his enemies, that he might see and bless his beloved boy once more, ere he depart."

Taking his son's cold hand in one of his, he used the other to search for a pulse on the boy's throat. In vain. "My boy is gone to his God. Let us pray," he said. As he thanked the Lord for the loan of the boy and for taking him at this time to avoid the travails to come, the women tended to the child, their tears bathing his head.

Austin then told the women how, following the loss of his guards over the precipice, he had retraced his steps in the hope of seeing his son one more time. He was confident of his guards' safety: so deep was the snow, he was sure they would sustain only bruises. Accordingly he expected his visit to be brief, with the men soon returning for him.

In the meantime a coffin was made ready for the boy. It was moved to the now-vanished village of Mortontown, where an uncle of Samuel's tenanted a small farm. This farm bordered the graveyard and on the second night after his death, the boy's burial took place in the quiet secret of the night.

At Austin's direction, a second coffin was kept empty in the house. As he explained to his wife and uncle, his plan was this. After appropriate modifications to enable a living body to spend some time in it, this coffin would provide ideal concealment should a search for him be made.

As he had anticipated, his guard did return. As was usual in such searches, they tested all possible hiding places by passing their swords through them, drinking, swearing and roaring as they went. However, even at their boorish worst they respected the coffin and passed out of the house leaving it unexamined.

At that time, the farm of Brownrig was tenanted by a Mr Halbert Hunter, known locally as Honest Hal. He was a dedicated Covenanter who had on many an occasion trekked up to 15 miles on a Sunday to hear Samuel Austin preach. Brownrig being so remotely located and far from even the nearest neighbour, he had to walk some distance to get anywhere for anything, and much of that walk through wild country.

This time, though, he set off to find Mr Austin to rescue him, risking all by offering refuge in his remote home. Sadly no one could help: there was no intelligence of the man or his whereabouts. But as he was passing Morton Manse, his horse took fright at some clothes frozen hard and swinging on a line. The animal reared up and threw him off, he landed badly and was hard bruised. He was taken to the farm of Mortontown, where the Reverend was staying. At first the occupants took care to keep Mr Austin and his family away, but the good Hal was eventually recognised, his errand ascertained and the two parties brought together, where they spent the evening in prayer and pious conversation.

The next evening saw the careful and difficult removal to Brownrig, done with as much secrecy as possible. But eyes and ears were everywhere, with tongues willing to talk. The following day, as Austin was addressing a group of local young men and women, they were surrounded by Dalziell's band of dragoons. Austin was finally captured without resistance.

On hearing what was happening, his sister rushed out in the direction of the sound, frantically calling on the men to spare her brother. Before anyone could act, her direction of travel brought her to the precipice at the edge of the farm; she fell over and, landing on her head, died instantly. Her brother saw the risk as she neared the edge. He struggled to get to her, but the soldiers held him fast. On witnessing the tragedy he uttered a scream, bursting a blood vessel and suffering a stroke which made it difficult to get him to the house.

Once inside, Mr Austin was put to bed. Dalziell appointed two men to remain as guards of the man he now adjudged to be dying, telling his men, "The de'il has his soul fairly in tow".

When the day came to bury the late Miss Austin, a cortege of mountaineers braved snow and storm to accompany her the not inconsiderable distance to Dalgarno churchyard. The soldiers in their turn did all they could to annoy and obstruct. They offered to carry the coffin, then withdrew their hands so that without grace or dignity it fell to the ground. They placed muskets between the feet of some of the company so as to trip up their heels. Such behaviour proved too much to be borne, and after the funeral, which it was eventually possible to hold, it was agreed that the much-recovered Mr Austin and his wife be conveyed away from the watchful eyes of the men.

But how could this be done?

After lengthy discussions, a course was determined. Twelve stout shepherd lads, armed with pistols and staves, were without warning to enter the door of Brownrig house, the bolt of which would already have been opened from within. They should then bind the demon guards, who were still working such dreadful mischief and cruelty. The minister and his lady were to be conveyed through the snow to the town of Moffat, about four miles away, to be concealed in a friend's house.

At the agreed hour the shepherds arrived, their task made easier by the fact that the soldiers slept. Mr Austin, though better, could not yet walk and had to be placed on horseback with his wife behind him, two men holding him up on each side as they crossed the moors to Moffat. Arriving at five in the morning, the couple were lodged for a time in a place of safety.

On returning to Brownrig, the young men found only charred wood and smoke to greet them. On learning of the flight, Dalziell had razed the place to the ground. His intelligence had arrived too late for him to stop them, and on arriving back at the farm he could not discern the direction of travel due to drifting snow and ice. In his fury and frustration, shots were exchanged with the remaining inhabitants, wounding one man seriously. On releasing his own captured guards he turned his vengeance on those who remained, setting fire to the thatched houses.

In Moffat it was now Mrs Austin who was not faring well. Her constant state of anxiety and the extreme cold had brought on a fever, and shortly after their arrival she died in her husband's arms, having exhorted him to persevere in the good cause he had undertaken before finally taking her leave.

In due course Mr Austin recovered from his stroke and spent his time in Moffat quietly recuperating in some peace and safety. During his recuperation he met with his brother-in-law, Mr Shiels, the minister of Kilbride.

It was now July and considered a good time to hold a general meeting, very, very privately on the confines of Lake Altrieve, sheltered all round by the moors of Yarrow and Ettrick clasped between the Tweed and Annan.

Austin's brother-in-law was considered fit to co-adjudicate the meeting. Local worthies, minor gentry and wealthy farmers agreed to pay for the communion. They also pledged to come armed, in case they were found and challenged for their actions.

A terrible storm raged, thunder, lightning and hail, as Mr Austin preached the sermon and Mr Shiels fenced the tables. After the storm had passed, the day cleared. The mist left Mount Benger's brow, and Bowhill looked out in soft and sparkling radiance. There was no sign of an approaching enemy, and the two clergymen returned with the shepherd Davie Dun to spend a night's sleep in his bothy.

By daylight next morning the bothy was surrounded by dragoons. Austin and Shiels were dragged out of bed. Mounted together on one horse without a saddle, their legs tied together under its belly, in this painful and ignominious state they were driven across the mountains towards Peebles.

Austin had not completely recovered from his stroke. He became so faint and weak that he could not sit, even when supported by a dragoon at each side on horseback, and the party were forced to lodge for the night in Peebles.

The next morning they were marched off again, this time to Edinburgh, to appear before the Lauderdale Council. After close questioning, they were banished to the shire of Angus. It was made crystal clear to them that if they were found South of the Tay they would, without further delay or consideration, be taken up and executed as traitors.

In fact, all the 10 ministers of the Presbytery of Penpont, with the exception of Black of Closeburn and Wishart of Keir, had refused to conform. They, along with nearly 400 ministers, mainly from the South and West of Scotland, had been forced to fly their homes and flocks. Mothers carried their infants through the snow, whole families wailed. Those good enough to offer food or shelter were themselves liable to fines or worse.

In many cases these clergy were conveyed in droves beyond the Tay, compelled to emigrate to foreign lands or to take up their abode with the curlews and red hawks of the lake and the mountain. Many never returned, stolen from their only known and useful roles. The scale of this cruelty and tragedy was biblical.

Some two decades passed before Austin was able to return to his parish. And he found it much changed, as he recorded in his notebook:

"August, 1689. It hath pleased the Lord to restore poor old useless Samuel Austin to his people; but where are they? Twenty years have made a sad event and reckoning here. The child has attained to manhood; the man has disappeared, or labours under the infirmities of age; and many have been removed, not only by death but by duty. They have removed, in the course of God's providence, to other parishes, and even to other lands; and my flock is changed. I feel no heart in preaching to these new faces. O Lord, let me arise and go hence! I am alone, in an altered world of which I am weary. My house is desolate. My child, my wife, my sister, all, all gone on before. And fain, o guid Lord, wad I follow: now let thy servant depart and sleep in peace."

In the kirkyard of Penpont, at the west end of the church, there is a monument with the following inscription:

"Here lies the worthy and godly Samuel Austin, forty-five years minister of this parish, nineteen of which years he was banished by ungodly men from his dear flock and sorely persecuted for the truth and for presbytery's sake. God was pleased to restore him again at the period of the Glorious Revolution and he continued to the day of his death, 25th April, 1694, faithfully though in much bodily weakness, to administer to his loved and loving flock. "

Retold by Denise Bradshaw

The grave of Samuel Austin at Penpont Parish Kirk

The Trials of the Rev Samuel Austin
Background

This Tale is one of 47 attributed to Professor Thomas Gillespie, of which 25 appeared under the heading Gleanings of the Covenant. Gillespie, Professor of Humanity at the University of St Andrews, contributed numerous articles both in prose and verse to the leading periodicals of the day, including essays in *Blackwood's Magazine* and *Constable's Miscellany*. In 1822 he published a volume of sermons entitled *The Seasons Contemplated in the Spirit of the Gospel.*

Professor Thomas Gillespie 1777-1844

His account of the persecution of Samuel Austin is set in the 'Killing Times', when episcopacy was being forced on the Presbyterian Scots by the restored King Charles II. In a footnote to the story, Gillespie cites a description of this period in *Sketches of Scottish Character*, a series in *Blackwood's Magazine*:

"Sad time indeed, oh most detested time, When vice was fealty, and religion crime; When counsellors were traitors to the state; A chancellor's authority was fate And Scotland felt the grasp, o'er muir and dale, Of cruel, beastly, turncoat Lauderdale; When Grierson stepped abroad in human gore, The peaceful peasant butchered at his door; And cruel Graham, and merciless Dalziell, In nightly rendezvous enacted hell."

This was not only a religious struggle but also a civil one, ending the concept of the 'divine right of kings' and beginning a transfer of power to the people. It was a period of civil disobedience erupting into civil war that spanned almost 100 years both before and after the Civil War and Commonwealth of Oliver Cromwell in England.

In 1597, in his books *The True Law of Free Monarchies* and *Basilikon Doron*, King James VI of Scotland had asserted the divine right of kings and his determination to have no competing authority in the land. In his eyes, the Kirk was a competing authority, with its Presbyterian policy of rule by an assembly of ministers and lay members independent of the state or any hierarchy.

Succeeding to the English throne in 1603 as James I, he believed that Presbyterianism was incompatible with monarchy: "No bishop, no King". By skilful manipulation of both Church and state, he steadily reintroduced parliamentary and then diocesan episcopacy. By the time he died in 1625, the Church of Scotland had a full panel of bishops and archbishops. General Assemblies met only at times and places approved by the Crown.

The differences between episcopacy and Presbyterianism lay at the very heart of what motivated the Covenanters. Charles I inherited from James a settlement in Scotland based on a compromise between Calvinist doctrine and episcopal practice. Lacking the political judgement of his father, he upset this by moving into more dangerous areas. Disapproving of the 'plainness' of the Scottish service, he contrived with William Laud, Archbishop of Canterbury, to introduce the kind of liturgical practice in use in England.

The centrepiece of this new strategy was the *Prayer Book* of 1637, a modified version of the Anglican *Book of Common Prayer*. Although this was devised by a panel of Scottish bishops, Charles' insistence that it be drawn up in secret and adopted sight-unseen led to widespread discontent. When finally introduced at Edinburgh's St Giles Cathedral, it caused an outbreak of rioting with the probably apocryphal exhortation of Jenny Geddes, said to have thrown her stool at the pulpit, crying "Whae daur say a mass in my lug?".

The insurrection spread across Scotland.

The National Covenant, demanding a free Scottish Parliament and General Assembly, was signed by thousands of Scots, nobles and commoners alike, on 29 February 1638 in Greyfriars Kirkyard. Copies were sent around the country and to London. Some signed in their own blood. It included a confession of faith asserting the Presbyterian Church's freedom in Scotland and its loyalty to the King:

"From the knowledge and conscience of our duty to God, to our king and country… we promise by God to continue in obedience of religion (Protestant and Presbyterian)."

In November 1638 the General Assembly in Glasgow, the first to meet for 20 years, not only declared the *Prayer Book* unlawful but went on to abolish the office of bishop itself. The Church of Scotland was then established on a Presbyterian basis. Charles' resistance to these developments led to the outbreak of the Bishops' Wars.

Charles I had hoped to destroy the Covenanters. But in 1643, during the English Civil War, the Scots entered into a Solemn League and Covenant with the English parliamentarians under Cromwell to achieve reformed religion, the Westminster Confession of Faith being agreed by both. This document remains a standard of the Church of Scotland.

By 1646, England's civil war was ending in victory for Parliament. Charles tried to persuade the Scots to help him against the English parliamentary forces, but the Covenanters would only agree to assist him if he established Presbyterian church government in England.

The King refused and the Scots let him to fall into the hands of Parliament. Initially they had been loyal to the King, but the Stuart monarch's sheer intransigence forced their hand.

After Charles' execution, the Scots were angered by the unilateral English decision to execute a monarch shared by both kingdoms, and a Scottish Stuart monarch at that. So they proclaimed the exiled Charles II as king, one week after his father's execution, in the hope of negotiating with him to secure 'a Covenanted king'.

Cromwell's fear of a Scots invasion of England to restore Charles II and impose Presbyterianism prompted his own invasion and occupation of Scotland in 1650. His victory at the Battle of Dunbar, followed by the capture of Edinburgh, meant Scotland was now under English rule. But after Cromwell's death in 1658, the Commonwealth did not survive; and in 1660 Charles II was restored to the throne.

In 1661 he repudiated the National Covenant. The following year, the Covenant was torn up and Charles' own bishops and curates were appointed to govern the churches. Some 400 nonconforming ministers were ejected from their parishes. At first, the authorities tolerated them preaching in houses, barns or the open air, in unofficial services known as conventicles. But it was soon realised that the people's resolve was such that they would not attend the King's appointed Episcopalian ministers' services. The first attempt at limiting attendance at conventicles was made in 1663; by 1670 attendance became treasonable and preaching at them a capital offence.

Samuel Pepys, an assiduous church attender, noted in his diary the outlawing of conventicles and the gaoling of Quakers and Papists, without obvious comment but with a hint of approval. An ardent royalist, he saw the Covenanters as dissidents to be suppressed.

The years of warfare and persecution between monarch and people reached a peak in what became known as the 'Killing Times', when the King tried by force of arms to impose his will on the Scottish people.

Troops were ordered to break-up and prevent conventicles. People were fined for failing to attend church, and absentees' names were listed. By 1666, the persecution of listed non-attendees by soldiers was so harsh that the country became increasingly restless.

Open rebellion broke out when the villagers of Dalry in Galloway witnessed soldiers roasting an old man with branding irons. It had not been planned, but numbers flocked to the cause and a spontaneous march took place in horrific November weather, via Lanark towards Edinburgh. The exhausted Covenanters were ultimately defeated at Rullion Green in the Pentland Hills, when an army of 3,000 led by General Tam Dalyell routed the meagre band of 900 protestors. A hundred were killed on the battlefield and 120 taken prisoner, marched to Edinburgh and charged with treason and rebellion. It is estimated that a further 300 Covenanters escaped, but died or were slain on their way home

This is the background to the Tale.

A generation or more of Scottish people were persecuted, rendered destitute and, in some cases, transported as slaves to the Americas or executed on the orders of their king for no reason other than their wish to worship after their own beliefs.

Of those most involved in attacking the Covenanters and brutally suppressing people attending conventicles, the most notorious was John Graham of Claverhouse, known to his enemies as Bloody Clavers. Another was General Tam Dalyell, the victor at Rullion Green, who features in *The Trials of the Rev Samuel Austin*.

The late Tam Dalyell MP, a direct descendant of the General, had a theory that his ancestor was mistakenly blamed for the events in the Tale, having taken no part in attacks on the Covenanters after the battle of Rullion Green. It may be that he was confused with a lesser-known figure called Robert Dalziel (Dalyell) of Glenae, who was commissioned to enforce the law throughout Dumfriesshire, or a Captain John Dalziel of Mar's Regiment of Foot who 'harassed much in Annandale'.

The terror campaign against the Covenanters came to an end with the Glorious Revolution when, in a bloodless coup, William of Orange and his wife Mary became joint rulers of the United Kingdom.

This put an end to the House of Stewart, which had ruled Scotland for over 300 years and England, Scotland and Ireland for 86 years. James II and his son, Charles, tried to reclaim the crown in the Jacobite risings of 1689, 1715 and 1745, but were unsuccessful. The new King William was persuaded by his advisers, principally William Carstares, a Scottish minister who had become his friend in Holland, to accept Presbyterianism as the established church in Scotland. In 1690, Parliament re-established Presbyterianism in Scotland, and to this day the Church of Scotland, the Kirk, remains a Presbyterian Church.

The harrowing story of Samuel Austin, written nearly 200 years after the events, shows how deeply the Covenanting times, and the violence and bloodshed associated with them, were burned into the psyche of the Scottish nation, influencing attitudes and opinions in the centuries that followed. The vein of anti-establishment feeling that can still be found in the Scottish character may have its roots in accounts such as *The Trials of the Rev Samuel Austin.*

Background by Dr Michael Fenty

The Domestic Griefs of Gustavus M'Iver

Gustavus M'Iver, a mountain of a man! Six feet five inches of leathery skin and hardened sinew: a veteran of the Peninsular Wars and a survivor of the Siege of St Sebastian. While he cut down many Frenchmen in wondrous acts of sheer killing, he was also noted for an unexampled adroitness in the art of carving meat both for himself and others; for as well as being a soldier, Gustavus was in charge of the entire Mess, a post of honour he had acquired for his undisputed superiority in culinary lore.

So, here is Gustavus, the hero of the Tale: as good a man as ever God put breath in, retired from the wars and home in Edinburgh's Canongate filled with glory. A man of huge stature, with an authority derived from his willingness to hold his tongue and rely on silence in his dealings with his fellow men.

But as the giant Goliath was slain by the shepherd boy, David, so was Gustavus felled by a mere toy of a thing. Cupid, the blind boy, in some mischievous attempt to keep up a reasonable mean size among human creatures, paired our hero with Julia Briggs.

Julia, a little milliner, only as big as one of Gustavus' huge limbs, had been a standing toast among the city's smaller men of fashion. But she had her eye on Gustavus: motivated not by love but rather by his ability to provide her with a home and the protection of his huge stature.

Gustavus had already decided he would like a wife, and the sight of Julia skipping along, twisting and wriggling, twirling and twinkling, proved his downfall. Cupid's tickling shaft scored a bull in the leathery organ of his heart. Tease-Julia was well aware of the effect she was having on the poor besotted mountain of a man as she displayed her ankle in her dancing walk, and took saucy glances over her shoulder to check that he was following her. When she reached her mother's house she displayed herself at a window with her cap off and her hair loose while Gustavus stood outside, lost in the throes of hopeless passion.

Like all lovesick swains in history, Gustavus lost sleep and appetite. A man who had thought nothing of consuming pounds of flesh at a sitting was now rendered hollow-eyed and empty-bellied by Julia's wiles. A mere three days after falling for Julia, he presented himself at her door and proposed marriage as quickly as it takes to down a pull of jolly good ale.

No sooner proposed than job done. They were married a week later and Gustavus was to prove the truth of the old adage, "Marry in haste, repent at leisure", as the tiny tease set about taming her man to suit her ways. So began the domestic griefs of Gustavus M'Iver.

Illustration by Claire Jenkins

Gustavus' joy on his wedding day barely showed on his leathery features. In fact, the only extraordinary emotion that crossed his face matched that seen just once before, when he hewed down so unmercifully the French at St Sebastian. So did he see his marriage as a conquering of his wife? Certainly, in his new domestic environment Gustavus was still a soldier, his orders to Julia were more martial than marital. But getting a wife is a small matter in comparison to the ruling of her; and Julia was no Kate, nor Gustavus a Petruchio.

To place his wife under his thraldom and subordination he decided she alone should minister to his every want and comfort. He promptly dismissed his servant, thus saving on wages and keeping his wife, he hoped, busy and occupied in case Satan should find other activities for her potentially idle hands.

Now Gustavus was well able to look after himself. He had been an excellent cook and could keep his linen in good order, washing and repairing his clothes as need be. These were the two main demands for his comfort, and his own expertise in these areas was indisputable. But Julia had given up her work as a seamstress and had no intention of cooking. She had married simply for her own convenience: his needs for pure linens and well-cooked victuals were not going to concern her unduly.

However, she had no intention in engaging in open warfare with him. So she became a professional incompetent, spoiling every piece of domestic labour to which she applied her hands. It was clear that Gustavus should have been the wife and Julia the husband.

Gustavus was, in his way, a perfectionist who loved good eating and clean linen. He was so annoyed by Julia's incompetence that he made his first mistake, taking the sovereignty of the kitchen on his own shoulders. He was thereafter seen bibbed and armoured in his apron, washing and dressing his own linen better than any washerwoman that danced in a trough in the village of Duddingstone.

Julia fell into the habits of idleness he had hoped she would avoid by caring for him. She was well fed and looked after, so what did she do? Unbeknown to Gustavus, she became a hardened whisky drinker.

Tucked away in the Edinburgh closes, she had access to dram shops and secret stills and swallowed good whisky in choppins. She had no fear of Gustavus, as he still loved the wicked imp. And she knew her rights, in that Gustavus could not turn her away without supporting her; nor could he beat her, as she would leave him and sue him for alimony. Furthermore, she knew he loved her.

Illustration by Susan Plover

So there was Gustavus, cook and servant to a manipulative baggage. Not only cook and servant but now, because of her excessive drinking, also her nurse. A man whose very look has spread terror around him had been reduced to ministering to one of the smallest women that ever drew breath and one of the greatest drunkards that ever drank whisky.

The time had come for Gustavus to actually start to think: an operation of marvellous difficulty to him. The first result of his cogitations was simply to stop her supplies. This proved useless, as Julia still managed to drink and demand his ministrations as a nurse. So he had to think yet again. The second result was to imprison her in her room. He overlooked the power of her voice and the window!

Julia yelled for the constables, whose assistance was duly given. Gustavus was told to his teeth that he had not a jot of right in imprisoning his wife. Julia celebrated her freedom by becoming more intoxicated than ever.

His third attempt to curb her was to saturate her with whisky, hoping she would either become sickened by surfeit or die. Julia was able to avoid either outcome by taking only what was good for her while at the same time thanking him for his kindness and allowing him to assist her drunken self to bed nightly.

So Gustavus worked out a new method of controlling her potations; he would remove her from the temptations of the city to a remote part of the country. The cottage he chose was truly isolated: no neighbours, no dram shops and no other house for miles around. The only human contact was with a carrier who passed with any necessary provisions.

All went swimmingly for six whole weeks. Julia remained sober but still made Gustavus continue his domestic duties. Deprived of her drams she spent her time reading novels. One day, confident of his control over his wife, Gustavus took himself off for threequarters of an hour's striding about in the hills, only to arrive home to find his wicked enchantress comatose on the floor more drunk than she had ever been.

Gustavus was more than puzzled as to where his imp had acquired her supply. The carrier had not passed for a week, and a search of the house revealed no source of liquor. He was obliged to shrug it off as one of life's great mysteries and hope it was an isolated slip from grace. However, Julia did not remain sober. Every two or three days she was as bad, if not worse, than she had ever been in the midst of the dram shops in the City of Edinburgh.

The mystery deepened. A further extensive search of the house revealed nothing, the inhabitants for miles around were questioned and no one had ever been seen to call at the cottage. All was blank. Gustavus was mystified. Julia was smug.

This situation gave Gustavus ample time to brood. In selecting an isolated cottage he had deprived himself of contact with his fellow men. In the city he had been able to exchange views and smoke a pipe with companions, but here he had only Julia for company. His imagination ran riot and he began to think that his wife who sat and mocked him was in league with the Devil. He seemed unable to leave the house because it was certain that when he returned she would be drunk; and she had only to go out to return intoxicated.

Though Gustavus had been a fearsome and feared warrior, he did not frighten Julia. So, things now becoming desperate, he devised a desperate plan to terrify her: the next time he found her intoxicated he would put her in a coffin, and actually bury her in the earth.

Gustavus set about making a sturdy coffin, which he painted black and studded with white buttons taken from his old uniform. He stood the finished product in his bedroom, hoping to frighten his wife into total abstinence. Faint hopes! Julia laughed openly at him, claiming he would be hanged if he buried her alive. Three days later the pert minx was drunk again. This time, Gustavus did not put her to bed as was his wont but placed her in the coffin with a pickaxe on top and sallied forth into the countryside to carry out his burial threat.

His objective was a Stygian-dark wood some way from the cottage. There he found a ready-made hole nicely protected by bushes. What luck! No need for the pickaxe! He popped the lid on the coffin, which had plenty of holes in it so that Julia could breathe, and lowered the grisly object into the pit. Job completed, he went off home to cook his dinner, secure in the belief that when she awakened from her drunken stupor she would be so terrified it would instantly cure her of her taste for whisky.

What Gustavus did not know was that the hole in which he had left Julia was actually a subterranean distillery manned by two brawny Highlanders, Angus M'Guire and Donald M'Nair. Nor could he have known that this was where Julia had been obtaining her supplies.

Angus and Donald were busily at work when Gustavus was depositing his Julia-coffin, and totally terrified when they heard his movements. What they feared was what all illicit distillers feared: being discovered by the gaugers, the excisemen. They armed themselves with pistol and sword, prepared to kill before discovery. But not a gauger did they see, instead, a coffin descending into their secret spot. The faint light that glimmered round the cave was reflected by the rows of white buttons on the coffin and mortal terror seized them: terror 20 times more than if they had seen the ghost of a murdered exciseman.

Original illustration from *Wilson's Tales of the Borders*

They remained frozen to the spot until Donald, the bolder of the two, moved forward to prise open the coffin lid. There, revealed, was the corpse of their customer Julia: "Murtered by Gustavus, py Got!", and "Puried here to hide the plack, purning shame".

They were now on the horns of a dilemma: what to do with the corpse? After prolonged discussion they decided to wait for dark and then give Julia a decent burial. After all, they did not want to be thought to be "murterers o' the puir cratur".

To give them courage for the deed they fell to drinking their own spirits by the side of the coffin, and lamenting the unhappy fate of their former visitor. In the past they had enjoyed much fun and frolic with the saucy Julia, so they passed a jolly time sitting beside the coffin drinking steadily and musing about life and death generally, as frequently happens on funeral occasions.

As darkness fell they were well-flown with their own product. They had just proposed a toast to "the good cratur's soul" when Julia opened her eyes. Unaware of her situation, she held out her hand for a glass of the whisky she saw them drinking.

HORROR! Twenty ghosts in their winding sheets could not have produced a greater sensation. Donald and Angus threw down their quaiches and, screaming with terror, retreated to the farthest recesses of the dark abode.

Their terrors were matched by those of Julia. Though still not fully sober, she realised she was in a coffin, thought that she was truly dead and buried, and believed she was in the region appointed for the wicked daughters of men. Convinced that she had seen her friends Donald and Angus, she now believed that they too were dead and damned. Accepting her lot with some equanimity, she called out to them, demanding a drink to cure her thirst.

The two Highlanders soon realised that she was indeed alive. Julia remembered Gustavus' threat and, amidst a deal of laughter and drinking, explained everything. The irony! To cure his wife of her love of whisky, Gustavus had buried her in a distillery.

Meanwhile, what of Gustavus? He made himself a good dinner, complacently believing his cure would work. To make sure Julia would awaken in her subterranean quarters and be duly terrified into abstinence, he waited just over six hours before setting forth to exhume her. He knew he would be able to raise the coffin as he had left ropes around it. But, arriving at the woodland pit, he could see no sign of the ropes. Nor could he see any glimpse of the coffin as he peered into the hole.

Even poking round in the hole with a stick revealed no sign of the coffin. And no answer came when he shouted her name, although he seemed to detect faint sounds of laughter. He now grew frantic. Realising that he might have lost her forever, he suddenly loved her again! He was convinced that Julia had been stolen by some mysterious underground forces and his conscience began to trouble him. As darkness fell he returned home with the blackness of the mystery enveloping his brain.

Questions would be asked! The carrier, who had seen the coffin through the window, asked Gustavus with a knowing look where Julia was. Gustavus now realised that he might well have to face a murder charge. It was clear that tongues had begun to wag, for two days after Julia's disappearance local folk began to pry about the house. Gustavus grew daily more afraid: unable to eat, fearful of the fate that could await him on the scaffold and expecting any minute a visit from the authorities.

And now, what fresh Hell? A visit from his mother-in-law, with two of her pals in attendance! Gustavus saw them coming, saw the carrier stop to talk to them, knew he could not account for Julia's absence and promptly fled, locking the cottage door behind him. From afar he watched them trying to break into the cottage and, overwhelmed with shame that he, a slayer of Frenchmen, a hero of St Sebastian, should fear three old women, determined to accost them manfully.

When they saw him coming they shouted that he was a base and bloody murderer. Julia's mother, egged on by the carrier, demanded to know where the coffin was and whether her daughter was alive or dead, even accusing him of having eaten her. Gustavus was lost for words, so they set about him physically, scratching his face, pulling his hair, knocking him down and trampling on him. Our hero stood this only for a short time until valour returned and he got to his feet ready to do battle. The women called upon the carrier for help, but he took to his heels.

So they calmed Gustavus down with soothing words and eventually they all went off together to see where he had buried his wife. He showed them the hole, telling them that she had been there for three whole days. The women set about wailing and crying when, quite suddenly, Julia popped her head up out of the ground.

When she saw them all, she roared with laughter. After three days with Donald and Angus, she was as drunk rising from the ground as she had been when Gustavus had buried her. She ran, or rather, staggered, to her husband's arms and the pair embraced for at least three minutes.

Gustavus took her home, hoping to find out what had happened while she was in the bowels of the earth. But Julia gave no secrets away, not to her husband nor to her mother. From that moment Gustavus gave up any more attempts to cure Julia's irregular habits, contenting himself with the evil lot of a bad wife. He accepted that only death could now separate them.

> *He cooked, cleaned and suffered her whiskery ways –*
> *From then and right on to the end of his days.*
> *Julia had her man on a very tight tether –*
> *He's yoked now to her forever and ever!*

Retold by Christine Fletcher

The Domestic Griefs of Gustavus M'Iver
Background

The Domestic Griefs of Gustavus M'Iver is one of the 79 tales written by Alexander Leighton. Leighton was among 18 identified contributors who continued the Tales after Wilson's death in 1835. As editor, he was also responsible for the publication of the collected works. The Gustavus M'Iver Tale appeared in Volume 19 of the Walter Scott collection of 1869.

Leighton's exuberant style is apparent in this Tale in his many references – medical, classical, biblical and literary – reflecting his own background in medicine and the church. His hyperbolic, often whimsically extended images may seem a little overworked for modern readers; but his skill as a storyteller is evident in the way he moves smoothly from episode to episode, and the precision of his characterisation.

Even minor characters assume a life of their own. For example, his presentation of the carrier – who nosey-parkers into Gustavus' situation when Julia is 'buried' but disappears "the moment he saw there was a chance of battle" with the giant Gustavus. Likewise Donald and Angus, the illicit Highland distillers, who come alive through Leighton's use of phonetic speech. "Ochone!" exclaims Angus when the pair of them think Julia is dead, "Put this is a tam pad world. We mun hae a quaich to keep up oor courage."

Leighton sets the date for the action following Gustavus' retirement from the Army at the end of the Napoleonic Wars in 1815. He mentions that Gustavus had seen action at the Siege of St Sebastian, which took place between July and September 1813. Gustavus retired to the Canongate in Edinburgh with a fine reputation: Leighton stresses his huge stature and comically compares it with the tininess of Julia Briggs, the object of Gustavus' matrimonial intentions.

In a comic reversal of the situation in The Taming of the Shrew, Gustavus finds himself with a wife who not only cannot minister to his demands for 'good victuals and clean linen' but, through having too much time on her hands, becomes a hardened whisky drinker.

Edinburgh at the turn of the 18th century had eight licensed distilleries and more than 400 unregistered stills. So Julia has a ready supply. Removing her to an isolated cottage proves only a temporary solution: soon Julia is getting her supplies from an illicit, underground still.

At this time illicit spirit – on which no duty was paid – was recognised as 'the common man's best cash crop'. The duty paid on liquor was an important source of revenue for financing Britain's wars. The war with France led to a trebling of duty and the many legal sources of income in the Highlands such as crofting, fishing and droving were affected by recession. As a result, the money made from illicit distilling became a lifeline for many families.

In the 1800s illicit distilling was an accepted means of paying rent for a farm. Many landowners supplied barley to their tenants which, when converted into spirit, was returned in lieu of monetary rent. The 'draff', or leftovers from the distilling process, was a valuable feed for cattle. It was noted that 'the higher the duty to be paid, the greater the gain and the stronger the temptation'. The scale of the problem was such that in the 1820s as many as 1,400 illicit stills were being confiscated every year.

It is not entirely clear where Leighton sets his story. He mentions the Canongate in Edinburgh, but the isolated cottage is only vaguely located. When Julia awakens in her coffin and realises

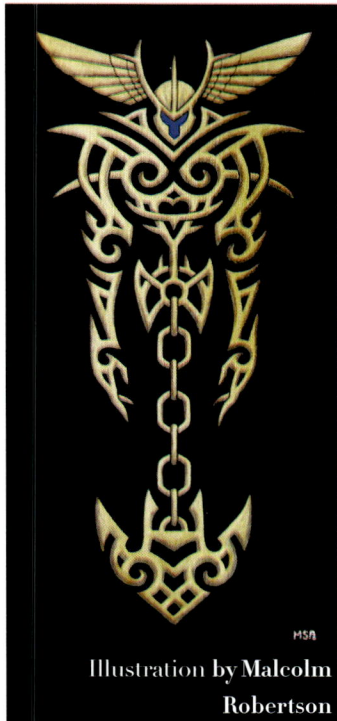

Illustration by **Malcolm Robertson**

she has seen her two distilling suppliers, she says: "When I saw them with the quaichs in their very hands, as I have seen before in the distillery in the wood of Balmaclallan". Balmaclellan exists; it is a village in Kirkcudbrightshire, but there is no record of illicit stills in the area. It is more likely that Leighton had in mind Balmenach on Speyside, which "in days gone by" had been the "haunts of smugglers who were pretty numerous in the district, and whose romantic history has been the subject of many numerous tales". The term 'smugglers' referred both to those who traded in whisky and also to the distillers themselves.

A description of one still in the area ran thus: "A double-arched cavern dug deep into the hill… it possessed an underground spring, wherein the little coil or worm which condenses the precious spirit was laid". There seem to be similarities here with the pit where Julia is 'buried' in the Tale. In the wild and remote country round Glen Livet there were said to have been at least 200 illicit stills. As well as the availability of barley, pure water and peat for firing the stills, the isolation of the area made it attractive for illicit distilling. This, then, could well have been the area where Leighton set his story.

Information from: *The Secret Still – Scotland's Clandestine Whisky Makers* by Gavin D Smith (2002).

Background by Christine Fletcher

"...manned by two brawny Highlanders, Angus M'Guire and Donald M'Nair."

Illustration by Jo Hart

Thomas of Chartres

Berwick-upon-Tweed, Winter 2017

John Wilson, editor of the *Berwick Advertiser*, is in his bright new office looking out over the Tweed towards Spittal, Holy Island and, off to the left, Scandinavia and Russia. He scans the contents schedule for the *Revival Edition of Wilson's Tales*. Three volumes so far, and a fourth to prepare! More Tales to be brought up to date – starting with *Thomas of Chartres*. Looking through his notes, he finds his original synopsis:

> 1298. Sir William Wallace is on board a Scottish vessel off the Isle of Man. Wallace, a larger than life figure, is Governor of Scotland, at war with Edward I of England and seeking Scottish independence.

> A vessel appears out of the fog. It's the formidable pirate, Thomas of Chartres. Wallace is up for a fight. He overpowers Chartres, but spares him once he realises that they were Crusaders together. Chartres has been exiled by the French king, Philip IV, also at war with Edward I. Scotland seeks alliance with France. Chartres confesses he is actually a de Longoville, and that he is happy to join Wallace and Scotland in fighting England, in the cause of justice.

Chartres then explains how he fought with Louis IX, the previous King of France, and then for his brother Charles: "Charles was a ruthless opportunist, determined to conquer Sicily. I joined him, hoping to gain land and status so that I could marry my sweetheart Agnes. Unfortunately her family expected her to marry the wealthy and powerful philanderer Lothaire Languedoc who, in cahoots with Charles, slandered me. I was arrested and condemned to death. I escaped, eloped with Agnes – and since then I have been at odds with Charles, and with Lothaire. I had planned to return to Palestine. But now I will fight for Scotland."

Wallace explains that, as King Philip owes him a favour, he will arrange to have Philip's accusation of treason against Chartres lifted. However, honour requires Lothaire and de Longoville to fight a duel.

The saloon bar of the paddle-steamer *Waverley*, Spring 2017

Wilson has joined the *Waverley* on a special excursion from Liverpool to the Isle of Man. He's in conversation with Lady Patricia, a handsome woman of middling years.

"So, Mr Wilson, what's this Tale about?"

"I can't say much just yet, but it has all the ingredients of a ripping yarn."

"For example?"

"A brave knight. A beautiful damsel in distress. Extreme weather. A rogue. Mistaken identity. Holy War. Territorial disputes. Foreign travel. A noble cause."

"Sounds intriguing to me. But what are you doing aboard the *Waverley*?"

"I wanted to get a feel for these waters. You see, in my original Tale, Thomas of Chartres, the hero is captured hereabouts in 1298 by Sir William Wallace. At first, Chartres is taken for a pirate; but he's not all he seems. To cut a long story short, he and Sir William join forces, and head for La Rochelle, that great naval base on France's Atlantic coast. Talking of which, you didn't happen to be on deck before breakfast?"

"As a matter of fact, I was. I'm an early riser, Mr Wilson."

"Then you probably noticed us passing the oil rig, the tug, the Russian destroyer, the British frigate, and that protest vessel, the *Vertipaxi Sunset*?"

"I did indeed: quite the little fleet! I wonder what they were up to?"

"Me too. I think it's helped me with my story."

"I'm intrigued, Mr Wilson…"

"Then perhaps, Lady Patricia, you might join me for dinner tonight? I may have more to tell you by then."

"It would be a pleasure, Mr Wilson."

The Irish Sea, just south of the Isle of Man, earlier that morning

The Russian destroyer *Vladimir* is escorting a Boris Class supertug, towing an oil rig north for drilling duty in the Arctic. Built in Odessa, she's come up through the Mediterranean. The *Vertipaxi Sunset* is tailing her, captain Sir Thomas Chartres at the helm. Yes, the same Thomas Chartres who is wanted by the CIA for alleged links to Islamic terrorists; by MI6 for allegedly leaking intelligence to *The Guardian* newspaper; and by the Russians seeking inside knowhow for their oil and gas drilling programme.

Until now he's been untouchable, protected by the laws of the sea while remaining in international waters. Now, in British waters, he's a sitting duck. *HMS Indestructible*, a Royal Navy Duke Class Type 23 Frigate captained by Jimmy Brichan, takes advantage of dense fog and its own sophisticated anti-radar and noise reduction technology to run-up alongside *Vertipaxi Sunset*, boarding her before the crew can resist.

The bridge of *HMS Indestructible*, shortly afterwards

Alongside *Indestructible*'s captain are Rear Admiral Sir William Wallace and his cousin, Brigadier Fergus Clelland. A big man with a big presence, Wallace is a close friend of Scotland's First Minister and a strong supporter of Scottish independence. Cousin Clelland is something hush-hush with GCHQ, an expert on surveillance.

As the *Vertipaxi Sunset's* skipper, Thomas Chartres, is brought onboard, Wallace summons him to a private meeting with himself and Brigadier Clelland. He orders coffee – and a tot of rum.

Wallace's quarters on *HMS Indestructible*

"So, it really is you Tom! I can't believe it's nearly 20 years since we were fighting together in Kuwait. But how did you end up working for Vertipax and in charge of the *Vertipaxi Sunset*?"

"All in good time, Bill. Before I tell you and Brigadier Clelland too much, I need to ask the same question: what brings you here?"

"Simple really. I'm a Scotsman through and through. My uncle was a regimental colonel in the Black Watch, taught me highland reels and how to pay the bagpipes when I was still in short troos. My hunch is that Brexit is going to end in tears, so I'm all for an independent Scotland. The USA has Downing Street in its pocket, manipulating the Atlantic Alliance: I see the dis-United Kingdom heading to be the 51st State. So I want Scotland out. And like my colleagues in NATO, I see a bigger threat than political or economic upheaval – and that's climate change. So in many ways we're in the same boat, you and I."

"The Auld Alliance all over again, eh?"

"I think we can help each other. Now tell me, Tom: why the change of name to Chartres? You're a de Longoville, aren't you?"

"Indeed, but I needed another identity. I've always loved Chartres and its cathedral – the principles and knowledge they embody, embracing classical, Christian and Islamic wisdom and technology. So I felt 'Sir Thomas Chartres' was right for my new image. True, some call me a spy, pirate and ruffian, but I like to think the cause I believe in is nobler than that. The knighthood may be a bit of a liberty, but it works wonders with officials. And you know, being a knight reminds me of all those chess games we played under canvas in the Kuwaiti desert, waiting for Saddam to make his move."

"You won most of them, I recall. Like you, I soon realised power and influence lie beneath the surface, away from the public gaze."

"I became disillusioned with the politicians. My time in the Middle East shocked me. I joined up because I thought the West was right, a just cause. Taken in by Bush and Blair – just like the old Crusaders, really. Human nature doesn't alter much. But now, I agree with you: climate change is the biggest threat to planet and people. I started doing the research. Then I got headhunted by Vertipax. It's no secret that they were inspired by Greenpeace: the two organisations have a lot in common, but Vertipax does more behind the scenes."

"Come on, Tom, admit it – you're spies!"

"Well, I won't deny that a lot of Vertipax work is undercover, infiltrating organisations we perceive to be a threat, and not just to the environment. Everything's connected. Drought and flooding bring famine, conflict and migration in their wake. I had a degree in petrogeology, so it wasn't hard for me to go undercover with the oilmen. I'd met a few in Kuwait. These guys make mega-millions from fossil fuels. They're not so much climate change deniers, they just don't care: it won't be their problem in a hundred years, let alone a thousand. Oil magnates, alt-right US politicians, Russian oligarchs, fundamentalists of any colour – they're all in the same game. As they see it, the planet will be toast eventually anyway, so why not make money while the sun shines? But at the expense of truth, justice, humanity, the beauty and diversity of nature? I don't think so."

"So, what was your Road to Damascus?"

"Well, first the ruthless, cynical way the oil industry worked. Either hand in glove with western governments or, worse, under the smokescreen of being aid agencies. But then there was one man: Lothario Languedoc. Remember him? He used the contacts he made with the UN peace-keeping mission to start gun-running. Then he moved into selling black-market oil. Languedoc connived in the murder of my old boss Louis Anjou – and tried to seduce my French girlfriend, Agnès. To make that easier he framed me as a terrorist, and had me banged up in gaol in Tunis. Agnès soon sniffed him out for the rat he is, and helped me escape. We went to ground for several years, in a crumbling ruin Agnès had inherited in the Charente Maritime. That's when we had our daughter, Bertha. But I've never forgiven Languedoc, and I will get my own back on him."

Just then the bridge called: "Superyacht to starboard, Sir William, thought you'd like to take a dekko..."

The bridge, *HMS Invincible*

"Talk of the devil! It's that Russky superyacht – all $800 million worth."

"Charles Anjou-Romanov," said Tom. "White Russian ancestry, family fled to Paris in the 1920s to escape the Bolsheviks. Murdered his cousin Louis when we were peace-keeping with UN. He'll be tailing me – on Languedoc's orders, no doubt."

At this point Clelland, who'd been listening intently, cut in: "GCHQ know you're working undercover for MI6, Tom. Nice work, by the way, cutting a deal with the baddies. But tell me, how do you pass the info across, given that the internet's as full of holes as a Manx trawlerman's nets?"

"Chess, Mr Clelland. Not any old chess, but a special version played in the Harz Mountains. We've developed a rather ingenious way of passing intelligence to each other during a game. You see, Languedoc and Anjou-Romanov need me: my years researching and campaigning in the Arctic mean my expertise is invaluable to them. But they'll be worried to think I'm in the hands of the Royal Navy."

"Yes, I see that," said Sir William. "Why don't we issue a press statement that we've arrested you, and you're imprisoned awaiting trial for… compromising NATO intelligence, perhaps?"

"I suppose that'll do for now. But imprisoned where?"

"Easy: Barlinnie, north of Glasgow. All the best rogues go there."

"So let's helicopter me off pronto, while that yacht is still hanging around to see it. Handcuff me to Cousin Clelland and stick me in an orange jumpsuit. I'll walk slowly when we get up to the helipad, so they can get some nice pics for their Facebook page."

Sir William shook Tom by the hand and looked him straight in the eye.

"We need to keep in touch, Tom. I'm due in Berwick-upon-Tweed tomorrow. There's something I haven't explained yet, about the Green Crusaders."

"The Green Crusaders? You know about them?"

"More than that: I'm closely involved. Now, should I let Agnès know what's happening? From what you've told me, as soon as she hears you're banged up in Barlinnie she'll be on the next flight to spring you."

"Yes, I'd be grateful if you'd do that. Especially as my esteemed creator is keeping an eye on us."

"I didn't think you were religious. Not after all you've been through."

"I mean a certain Mr John Wilson. You see that paddle-steamer over there, the *Waverley*? On board is said Mr Wilson. For reasons which will become apparent, we can't move on without him. I suggest you launch a boat pronto and pick him up; don't forget to ask his lady friend to join him. Oh yes, and a final word of advice – don't look surprised, whatever he says."

Sir William looked confused. "You really are a dark horse, Tom: I haven't a clue what you're talking about. See you in Berwick."

Sir William's quarters, *HMS Indestructible*

"Mr John Wilson? Sir William Wallace, at your service. Welcome aboard *HMS Indestructible*. And your companion…?"

"Lady Patricia de Longoville."

"De Longoville eh? Not Tom's cousin, by any chance?"

"You could put it that way, Sir William." Lady Patricia gave him a look that said, don't ask: he didn't, turning to John Wilson instead.

"So, Mr Wilson, you certainly are leading us a merry dance. Where next?"

"Good question. I've spent all morning wondering, whilst watching your maritime manoeuvrings. Very entertaining, by the way. My fellow day-trippers have been fascinated to see drama on the high seas. Not quite what I'd had in mind – but perhaps even better, Lady Patricia?"

"Oh quite so, Mr Wilson, absolutely!" Holding his eye a fraction longer than politeness required.

"So now comes the tricky bit, Lady Patricia: how to get our two lovebirds together and achieve the final denouement?"

Then, turning to Sir William. "Wallace, old chap, you won't walk off the edge of this page will you? Not yet anyway, I may need you again soon. Clelland, on the other hand, you can go. I think you'd better see de Longoville onto the helicopter."

"I already have, Mr Wilson, in fact he left a page or so back."

"Of course he did, silly of me to forget. Now, before we take this story any further, I think you'd better all sit down."

Mr Wilson perched on Sir William's desk, gesturing to Sir William and Lady Patricia to be seated.

"Last year, on a walking holiday in the Harz Mountains of Germany, I came across a village called Ströbeck, where they play a very unusual variety of chess – with 96 squares, and extra players called 'advisers', 'old men' and 'couriers'. Fascinating! Also just what I needed to set off the *affaire d'honneur* between de Longoville and Languedoc. Languedoc's in an awkward situation, remember. He needs de Longoville's expertise and thinks Tom has forgotten how badly he treated him. There is an annual tournament. I realised that the way it is set up makes it ideal for passing secret information from one side to the other. Unhackable, so far more secure than any encrypted electronic data. Knowledge is power and, as you know, information on fossil fuels is worth billions. So there's a lot at stake. But I'm not the first to work this out: apparently there are more spies than call girls in Ströbeck for the tournament. So we'll be heading there, but first we have to make an important detour – to Charente-Maritime."

Charente-Maritime, France

In La Forêt de Saint Sauvant, some 50 miles inland from La Rochelle, a tandem is making its way slowly up a narrow lane. An attractive young woman, still in her teens, is in front; an older woman behind, panting and sweating.

"So, Mum, what exactly is Dad doing, and when do you think he'll be back?"

"I wish I knew, Bertha. Probably hobnobbing with the great and the good. Could be Davos, Paris, London or New York. Wherever he is, we'll be the last to know. The broadband is so poor here, and as you keep telling me our mobiles won't work except in town. Sometimes I wish he'd never heard of Vertipax, or nuclear power, or global warming."

"Or ecology, or green living, or the Green Crusaders."

Bertha's mother nearly fell off the back of the tandem. How does she know about the Green Crusaders?

"Exactly Bertha, *précisément*. Leaving us out in the sticks, no car, not much money, the place falling down around our ears. I just wish Tom would listen to me when I remind him that we can't live on hot air."

"Oh Mum, you know he means well. He thinks everyone should adopt a simpler life to survive on this planet. That's why he's away campaigning so much."

"Quite so. And since you mentioned the Green Crusade, you'd better know the whole story. I'm feeling puffed out, so let's have a rest."

They sat at the roadside while Agnès explained that Bertha's father was a leading eco-activist, working undercover with a global oil giant. What's more, one of his so-called colleagues was an old rival for Agnès' heart: Languedoc. She'd heard that they were to fight it out in some bizarre chess tournament in Germany, a cover for exchanging classified information. She was waiting to find out more.

She didn't have to wait long, for just then a rather good-looking chap came gliding up the lane on an electric bike. "Good afternoon ladies! I'm sorry to trouble you, but I'm looking for Madame Agnès de Longoville – I gather she lives in this area."

Agnès gave Bertha a sideways look: this chap looks promising, I'll see if I can find out a bit more about him.

"Well, the name certainly rings a bell. I think I have her number in my address book. But who should I say is looking for her?"

"Clelland, Brigadier Fergus Clelland. You can tell her I have an important message from her husband, Sir Thomas Chartres, aka Tom de Longoville."

Well, that did it. Bertha burst into tears, and Agnès confirmed that she was indeed Madame de Longoville, explaining that they lived in the old stone tower in the distance. "It's about to rain, so why not join us for tea and some gâteau? It's a *spécialité de ma maison.*"

They just made it to the house before the heavens opened. Whilst Agnès bustled about preparing tea and gâteau, Bertha went to change. Clelland was left studying the books in the living room. One in particular caught his eye: *Wilson's Tales of the Borders.* His family boasted reivers on his mother's side, and he was a Walter Scott fan. He'd heard of Wilson, but never had a chance to read any of his work. He opened it at random:

"Towards evening the sun disappeared in a veil of impenetrable vapour, mottled with grey, ponderous clouds, betokening an approaching storm. The knight, resigned to the horrors of the storm, found a deserted hermitage, a cell like an Egyptian tomb, in the face of a low precipice. The thunder began to roll in louder and longer peals, when a loud scream of dismay and terror, blent with the infuriated howl of some wild animal, rose from the dell, and a young female, closely pursued by an enormous wolf, came rushing down the declivity, stumbled, and fell, swooning, into his outstretched arms..."

"Milk and sugar with your tea, Brigadier?"

Coming back to the here and now, Clelland looked up – and realised that Bertha was a strikingly beautiful young woman. Meanwhile, she was thinking: Mum's right! I wonder if we can persuade him to stay the night?

"Perhaps I shouldn't be going into town tonight after all, Mum," she said.

"Probably not – not in this weather. You will stay the night, won't you, Brigadier?"

"That would be much appreciated. It will give me time to tell you more of your husband's plans."

"They wouldn't have something to do with chess, by any chance?" asked Bertha. Now it was Clelland's turn to look nonplussed. "No need to say, I can see from your expression that they do. I'm looking forward to hearing more over supper. Mum, I'm just going down to the cellar to fetch a nice bottle of claret."

The Barracks, Berwick-upon-Tweed

"A Sir Thomas Chartres on the line for you, Sir William."

"Tom, you old rascal, I was hoping you'd ring. The Get Out of Jail Free card worked, then?"

"Like a dream – in fact, I never actually got to Barlinnie… but you don't need to know about that. So, what next?"

"You're due at Ströbeck in a couple of days' time. My job is to tell you what you need to know, and what you need to tell Languedoc… Not the same things, of course. The only way to do this without anyone else hearing us is face to face."

"When and where?"

"Here in Berwick. I'll see you on the old battery emplacement on the ramparts just past the Gymnasium Gallery. Noon tomorrow, don't be late."

Next day, noon, Berwick Ramparts

"So why Berwick-upon-Tweed?"

"It's complicated. Essentially, I need to be on English territory – but also, given the political sensitivities, close to Scotland. That meant either Carlisle Castle or here. Berwick was a no-brainer."

"To you, perhaps."

"If I need to get anywhere fast and undercover, I travel sub-aqua. The local lifeboat crew have all signed the Official Secrets Act. The lifeboat's fast, and we can rendezvous with the sub under cover of darkness. Couldn't do that in the Solway."

"Very neat. So, tell me more."

"As you know, Scotland is about to become independent. I'm working undercover for the new Scotland, trying to win over as many movers and shakers as possible. We're expecting the US to use Trident to pressurise the British Government into a deal securing American sovereign bases at Faslane, Holy Loch and a couple more I can't mention. Essentially, they'll be part of the US of A. But Trident is just a smokescreen. As you'll know well, the real action is oil and gas. Everyone thinks the North Sea is drilled out, but we know it's not. There are huge untapped reserves. Languedoc's lot need your expertise. But so does Scotland, and the planet. All those years you spent campaigning in the Arctic: there's a lot of money on your head. These are desperate times. You need to know that Scotland is heading-up a multinational consortium codenamed the Green Crusade. I can't say who they all are: some countries are still sitting on the fence. But sooner or later there'll be a showdown with the major powers. We need Languedoc out of the equation. You won't want to hear this, but apparently he's still got a soft spot for Agnès. That's why we wanted her and Bertha to join us in Ströbeck."

"Bait for Languedoc, eh?"

"Yes, I'm sorry."

"Don't be. Agnès and I've often talked about luring him into a trap. Seems like you're setting it up nicely, saves me a job. So count me in as a Green Crusader."

Sir William smiled. "I already have. Just this declaration of secrecy to sign, and you're one of us."

"My pleasure. Very happy to follow you and an independent Scotland anywhere!"

"Good. So the plan is, under cover of darkness we take a trip on the Berwick lifeboat. You'll be in Ströbeck in time for breakfast. I'm told the Café Gambit in the main square does very good Kaffee-crema and Apfelstrudel."

Market Square, Ströbeck, Germany

In the Gambit, Tom is reading the *Guardian Weekly*, a copy of *How to Win at Ströbeck Chess* unopened on the table. He's depressed and lonely – hoping Clelland has found Agnès and Bertha, and that he'll see them soon. It's not just climate change, but the state of the world in general that's getting him down. Humans! Why do they always end-up fighting one another, just because they can't agree? Politicians, businessmen, all the same – driven by greed, arrogance and ignorance. And all embodied in one person: Languedoc!

The next day: the chess tournament

It's played out in the Market Square, where the 96 squares are a permanent, central feature. The townsfolk are the pieces. Languedoc a black castle; and de Longoville a white knight, as you'd expect. Agnès is a 'courier', and Bertha an 'adviser'. The villagers not playing are seated in serried rows in a special pavilion, raked and raised so that they can see every move clearly. The pieces wear beautiful costumes, as if for a medieval joust. It's a tradition that the identities of the two players are kept secret, so they wear masks. They sit on special high chairs, rather like the umpires at Wimbledon, and shout out the moves. A black woman and a white man. For anyone not in the know, it's gobbledygook; but like any code, if you know it, it all makes sense. So de Longoville quickly recognised when black went for the Calabrian Countergambit, part of the Bishop's Opening: C23 – 1.e4 e5 2.Bc4 f5. White retaliated with the Four Pawns Gambit – what else could he do? C23 – 1.e4 e5 2.Bc4 Bc5 3.b4 Bxb4 4.f4 exf4 5.Nf3 Be7. But then black called for a courier to king's castle, and Agnès stepped onto the board, heading straight for Languedoc.

Yes, he was a little surprised to see her – but not totally. He thought she might still carry a torch for him. She slipped him the traditional gold envelope. He opened it, an ugly smirk spreading across his face. He sensed victory. A number of Ordnance Survey coordinates – he recognised one of them off the Scottish coast north of Scrabster. He'd get his boys to check out the rest. Then he turned the note over, looked at Agnès, and raised an eyebrow: Room 323, Hotel Bismarck, 21.30. Knock twice. Really?

Room 323, Hotel Bismarck

In Room 323 he found not one but two women – the younger one in a revealing evening gown – and a magnum of Champagne chilling in a silver bucket on the balcony. Languedoc had always thought Agnès beautiful, but the young woman beside her was a real stunner. He wasn't called Lothario for nothing, he reminded himself, mentally preparing his seduction routine – in chess code of course. The Greco Gambit, he thought, that should do the trick: C24 – 1.e4 e5 2.Bc4 Nf6 3.f4 Nxe4.

But Bertha was ready for this. She retaliated with her favourite, the Jerome: C23 – 1.e4 e5 2.Bc4 Bc5 3.Bxf7+ Kxf7. It worked like a charm. A couple of minutes later Languedoc was entertaining a gaggle of journalists outside the hotel. Not surprising, really, since he was dangling head-down from the balcony, suspended at the ankle by a pair of silk stockings, a suspender belt, a brassiere, and a G-string. Agnès was slowly drizzling the rest of the Champagne over him. Down below, de Longoville had rigged up a trampoline.

"You can drop him now, darling."

Agnès, nail-scissors at the ready, cut the bra strap. Languedoc bounced inelegantly a few times before being whisked into the stretch limo and off to the helicopter waiting nearby. The sun was just rising over the North Sea as the chopper dropped into the parade ground at Berwick Barracks. Sir William Wallace was there, preparing to interrogate.

Once Languedoc was behind bars, it was time for Clelland and Bertha to tie the knot and make themselves scarce. A quiet wedding, with Sir William as best man, then a retreat to a pele tower in the Borders. Apparently they're still there, living the good life, Agnès and Tom in a cottage nearby.

The Mersey

Waverley was making its majestic way up the Mersey, the setting sun behind it, the occasional belch of black smoke from its funnel – almost Turneresque. Mr Wilson and Lady Patricia had just finished their Solway supper in the First Class saloon – Manx kippers, Loch Arthur cheese, ginger beer.

"So what do you think, Lady Patricia?"

"Oh Mr Wilson, it's a charming story! You are such an inspired writer, and that last page is really quite racy. I can't wait for the next one!"

"You may not have to wait long – look! That superyacht has berthed. I think we'd better investigate, don't you, Pat?"

"Good plan, John – we'll make a good team!"

Retold by **Nick Jones**

The quotation on the statue's pedestal is by eighteenth century poet James Thomson. The Earl of Buchan loved Thomson's work, and built the Temple of the Muses at the bottom of the hill as a memorial to him.

Poetic tributes

The Earl himself wrote the words on the urn. Their style is perhaps a clue to his character.

The peerless knight of Elderslie
Who wav'd on Ayr's romantic shore
The beamy torch of liberty,
And roaming round from sea to sea
From glade obscure of gloomy rock
His bold companions call'd to free
The realm from Edward's iron yoke.

William Wallace at the Bemersyde estate, commissioned by David Steuart Erskine, 11th Earl of Buchan.

Made of red sandstone by John Smith of Darnick and erected in 1814, the monument portrays Wallace looking over the River Tweed.

It is inscribed:

> Erected by David Stuart
> Erskine, Earl of Buchan
> WALLACE
> GREAT PATRIOT HERO!
> ILL REQUITED CHIEF!
> MDCCCXIV

Thomas of Chartres
Background

Fate it surely was, when Andrew Ayre invited me to write the background to *Thomas of Chartres*. I am a Chartres. My great, great, great-grandparents on my mother's side were James and Elizabeth Chartres. I know this from the birth certificate of their son, William Chartres, born on 3 April 1839 in Berwick. Only the most fastidious of genealogists would take issue with the inescapable conclusion that I am a descendant of Thomas – that most noble, chivalrous knight of France's medieval court. I have French blood running through my veins. It explains so much: why hearing *La Marseillaise* tempers the iron in my soul; why I've never been fond of roast beef; and how it is that I can watch *Allo Allo!* without needing subtitles.

Thomas of Chartres is set in 1298. Though there is no hint of it in the Tale, this was a pivotal year in Scotland's first War of Independence against Plantagenet England. The war had started with the 1296 Good Friday massacre at Berwick – and apparently ended that summer with the removal of Scotland's king, John Balliol, into London captivity and the kingdom's capitulation to England's Edward I, Hammer of the Scots.

In August 1296, the Hammer held his Ragman Roll parliament at Berwick, where all the great and good of Scotland's aristocracy swore their feudal allegiance to him. All, that is, except for William Wallace – whose name does not appear on any of the 35 parchment skins that make up the Roll, and who in 1297 emerged from Ettrick Forest to defeat the auld enemy at the battle of Stirling Bridge. For a short while after the battle, Scotland was in the ascendant. Edward's colonial administration in Scotland collapsed, Wallace's Army of the Realm retook Berwick for Scotland, and Northern England suffered, and suffered again. It is this heroic, all-conquering Wallace that we see in *Thomas of Chartres*. We'll come to the Wallace of 1298, after the battle of Falkirk, presently.

Wilson's principal, possibly only source for his Tale is revealed towards its denouement. It is the epic poem of Braveheart – *Actes and Deidis of the Illustre and Vallyeant Schir William Wallace* – penned around 1477 by Blind Harry, a poet in the court of James IV of Scotland. The poem had been largely forgotten until 1722, when William Hamilton of Gilbertfield translated it into the Scottish vernacular of the time as *The Life and Heroick Actions of the Renoun'd Sir William Wallace, General and Governor of Scotland.*

So in 1834, when it is Wilson's turn to put pen to paper, we have a 600-year thread: a mid-19th-century version of an 18th-century translation of a 15th-century account of a 13th-century tale. Myth, legend, fact, fiction and embellishment are intertwined to such a degree that distilling *Thomas of Chartres'* historical truth, whatever that might mean, is a well-nigh impossible task – though hugely enjoyable nonetheless.

Blind Harry's Wallace is just shy of 12,000 stanzas, divided into 12 books. It starts with a brief account of the royal succession crisis in Scotland that led directly to the Hammer's bloody 1296 visit to Berwick. It ends with Wallace's 1305 execution. We first encounter Thomas in the opening chapter of Book IX. Wallace, we are told, has been invited to France to be feted by its king, Philip the Fair. Two days after sailing from Kircudbright with '50 stout Scottish gentlemen' – including four near-kinsmen of Wallace: two cousins, and Crawford and Clelland – Braveheart's single ship unhappily encounters "Sixteen great ships that boldly up did bear/ Ant towards them a steady course did steer/ In colour red, which with the sun shine bright,/ The sea all o'er illuminate with light".

The ships are those of Thomas the Red Reiver, 16 years a pirate following his banishment from the French court after by mischance killing a man with a single sword stroke. Upon the pirate being subdued by Wallace, the two men become bosom pals. They sail together to the French port of Rochelle, and from there to Philip's court – where Wallace's diplomacy secures a royal pardon for his new-found friend. They show their gratitude by joining the French king's Gascony War against (who else?) the Hammer. Their adventure successfully concluded, they sail to Scotland to continue the kingdom's fight for independence. Thomas remains an honorary Scot until and after Braveheart's death, which he laments with a warrior's promise:

> *"He never would depart from Scotland more;*
> *Nor yet his native land of France would see*
> *On Wallace foe, till he aveng'd should be".*

Wilson takes up Harry's tale and develops it. He gives Thomas a backstory as a crusader knight and a future including a part in the finest moment of Scotland's independence struggle: Robert the Bruce's Battle of Bannockburn.

The backstory. In June 1249, one of France's most revered kings, Louis IX, accompanied by 2,500 Templar and Hospitaller knights together with 5,000 crossbowmen and 10,000 sundry troops, set sail from Cyprus on the Seventh Crusade. Louis intended to follow the 'Egyptian Strategy' pursued by so many of his crusading predecessors: subdue Egypt first, then lead his forces into the Holy Land to secure Jerusalem for the Christian West.

The expedition started successfully enough. Damietta, a port on the Nile, fell quickly: a sure sign in the crusaders' eyes that they had God on their side. But as they travelled along the Nile delta towards Cairo and reached Mansura (Massouna in Wilson's account) their God abandoned them to disease – scurvy and dysentery in particular – and defeat. Louis was not spared; he yielded to illness in April 1250 and was taken prisoner during the retreat to Damietta. Freed a month later on payment of a ransom and the surrender of Damietta, he stayed for four years in Palestine before returning to France, where he spent the next decade and a half campaigning for funds and forces for another expedition. His wish was eventually granted. On 1 July 1250 he set sail from France for Carthage. On 25 August the crusade ended on his death, from dysentery.

Wilson places Thomas on the walls of Damietta, fighting alongside the best of his countrymen, and seeing the city handed back in the spring of 1250 as part-payment for his king's freedom. From there we leap forward to the spring of 1298, when Thomas and Wallace meet for the first time. Thomas' crusading years are, we are told, some 25 years behind him – implying that he entered retirement not long after Louis' fatal second expedition.

And this, unfortunately for the purposes of authenticity, presents us with a little difficulty: if we assume Thomas was a youthful, perhaps even teenaged, knight when he took his stand at Damietta, his memory of the event would have been disappearing rapidly into the distance when he made his piratical career change nearly 50 years later. Add to that Wilson's suggestion of a 1315 presence at Bannockburn, and his remark that Thomas lived 'a long and active life' begins to look like something of an understatement.

What of Wallace? In truth, his star shone brightly for only a very short period of time. If he did travel to France (and on balance it is probably true), it is extremely unlikely that he did so in the spring of 1298. Here's why. In May 1297 he burst onto the scene with his revenge killing of William Heselrig, the English Sheriff of Lanark and murderer of Wallace's wife. By the summer of that year he was the acknowledged leader of Scotland's first rising against the Hammer's colonial administration; and in September, as the victor at Stirling Bridge, he was rewarded with his appointment as sole Guardian of the Realm. By the end of October, his Army of the Realm had retaken Berwick for Scotland, and throughout the winter months of 1297 into early 1298 the same army indulged in the murderous harrying of the peoples of Northern England, east and west.

In response, an English army was mustered and headed north, Berwick falling into its hands in February 1298. By the spring, preparations were well under way on both sides – Edward in England, Wallace in Scotland – for the next confrontation. It came at Falkirk in July 1298. Wallace was defeated, and shortly afterwards resigned the Guardianship. He never again played a significant part in Scotland's fight for independence. If he did go to France it was no earlier than the autumn of 1299, on a diplomatic mission to seek Auld Alliance support. An increasingly marginalised figure, he became an outlaw in his own land by virtue of a Scottish parliament proclamation in 1304; and in August 1305 he was betrayed into the Hammer's clutches by a fellow Scot, Sir John Mentieth, Governor of Dumbarton Castle. Convicted at Westminster Hall, he was the same day hanged, drawn and quartered at Smithfield. Decapitated, his head was piked on London Bridge for all to see, and his four dismembered body parts were sent for display to Newcastle, Perth, Stirling and Berwick.

And what of the Berwick Chartres? William grew up to follow in his father's footsteps as a cooper, and like his father he married an Elizabeth. I am descended from one of their (at least) six daughters, Mary Jane. On her marriage, the surname disappeared from my branch of my family tree. But Thomas' blood is running still: *vive la France!*

Retold by Keith Ryan

"...when a loud scream of dismay and terror, blent with the infuriated howl of some wild animal, rose from the dell, and a young female, closely pursued by an enormous wolf, came rushing down the declivity, stumbled, and fell, swooning, into his outstretched arms..."

Original illustration from Wilson's Tales of the Borders

New Tales
from Berwick's Young Writers

When Wilson first started publishing his Tales, his original plan had been to publish 96 editions. Tragically, he died at the height of his success, before he got that far.

But the Tales continued, as they had become a great success. The main contributor after Wilson's death was Thomas Leighton, who also became editor. Aspiring authors from around Scotland submitted tales for consideration and over 20 authors subsequently had Tales published: some just a few and others several dozen. This brought a certain unevenness of style – one reason, perhaps, why *Wilson's Tales* have not stood out as a match for Walter Scott's works in their overall literary quality. But it also greatly broadened the range of subject matter – enhancing the richness and variety that make the Tales so fascinating even today.

With that in mind, we have been delighted to work once again with Berwick Rotary and the Berwick Literary Festival to invite new Tales to form part of this year's *Revival Edition* volume. For a second year we have done this through an open writing competition in local schools – which again inspired over 100 entries.

The winning entries have given us three new Tales. And while Wilson's originals were often loosely based on true events, our young winners have let their imaginations range freely. This year we have a modern take on the legend of St George and the dragon, a visit to Fairyland, and a first-person narrative from the brink of death.

I hope you enjoy these new Tales. We congratulate the young winners and hope the experience of becoming a published author will stimulate their enthusiasm for writing and literature in general. We look forward to hearing more of them in years to come!

Andrew Ayre

The Secret of the Closet Door
Young Writers Competition Winner

Once upon a time there was a happy little girl called Phoebe. She lived in a beautiful house with a white puppy called Snowflake. She had no brothers or sisters, she had a mum and a dad. She was 10 years old. Her fluffy puppy that was fluffy like a cloud was only six months old.

Chapter 2 A Secret Revealed

One hot summery day Phoebe was waking up from her big sleep. Snowflake was snuggled in with her. Phoebe got out of her bed and looked for clothes to wear. In the bottom of her wardrobe there was a magical but strange key. She picked up the strange key. Phoebe looked in her closet, there was a golden, sparkly door so she whistled Snowflake. She got the magical key and put it in the hole in the door, it fit, she turned it and turned it, and the magical door opened.

Chapter 3 A Magical Time

She went inside the door, so did Snowflake, and the door shut behind her. Loads of fairies were with her. One came up to her and said: "Hi, my name's Abbie. What's your name?" "My name's Phoebe."

They went further and further into Fairyland. Suddenly, Snowflake fell into the chocolate river. All the fairies dashed to Snowflake and quickly got her out. All the fairies said: "Would you like us to bath her for you?" "Yes please."

So off they went with Snowflake. The magic bridge appeared. "Come on, let's go!" "OK," said Phoebe, so off they went. Phoebe said: "Oh, look at those clouds, they're pink!" Abbie said: "Yes, they're made out of candy floss".

Chapter 4 Bad News Comes

In Fairyland everything was going fine. Abbie and Phoebe were having a picnic and then Snowflake came along with a letter in her collar. Phoebe took the letter out and it said: "Dear Abbie and Phoebe, I am the Evil Queen. I'm trying to get the jewels from the Golden Castle. I thought I would tell you because I know you cannot beat me!"

Abbie said: "Go be the hero and save the day!"

Everybody said: "She's a girl!"

Abbie said "OK, OK, I never meant to say that. OK, go be the heroine and save the day!"

So off she went with Snowflake. She came to a weird-looking tree: there was a button on it, so she pressed it. A beautiful dress was on her, she had a necklace that made her fly and Snowflake had a little tutu skirt on. They carried on walking.

Chapter 5 Getting to the Golden Castle

When Phoebe got there, the Golden Castle was black. But she wasn't in the wrong place, because the sign said: "Golden Palace". She went inside the door, and went to the room with the jewels in. The Evil Queen had actually took them. Phoebe did not realise that the Evil Queen had gone back to her lair, so off she went again. They finally got there. The Evil Queen was going to the forest to get some berries for her potions, so when she was away Phoebe ran into the house and quickly got the jewels. There was a black bat in a cage. Phoebe and Snowflake ran to the Golden Castle. They went inside the castle and put the jewels back in their place and put a lock round it, then went back to Fairyland.

Chapter 6 Going Home

She got back to Fairyland and Abbie came rushing to Phoebe and Snowflake. They all congratulated her. The Evil Queen came back and said: "I'm so sorry. I'll be good now." So they all had a tea party.

Then she said: "How are we going to get home?"

The fairies did their magic and sent her back home. She was so happy to be home but then she realised she could not see her best friends any more. Then the fairies made a window in the door and a hole in it, so they could talk to each other. It was time to go to bed by the time they got back, so Snowflake snuggled into her.

The end.

By Maddie Ferrell, aged 8

The Dragon and George
Young Writers Competition Winner

I was starving. Hibernation was over and I needed to hunt. Unfortunately, I had to wait until sundown before I could quench my thirst for fresh, human blood. After stretching out my enormous wings and growling loudly, I trudged through the scatter of bones that were crunching beneath my heavy weight, and curled up at the rearmost end of my hidden rocky hollow to watch as the sun gradually set in the West.

The sun had finally been completely dragged over the horizon when a loud rumble sounded out from my aching stomach. "Dinner time!" I thought greedily, as I flexed my wings and let out an almighty roar which caused the very ground beneath my taloned feet to tremble. As I soared through the darkened, never-ending sky a feeling of ecstasy spread through me with the joy of flying again; the flight over the Cheviot Hills was short, so I decided to stall for a while. A rich chuckle escaped my lips at the thrill of feeling the air rush past my scales and the gratifying aroma of Mother Nature fill my awaiting snout after the tedious months of hibernating throughout the bleak, bitter winter.

The abrupt scent of my unknowing prey caused my wings to falter; immediately, my desire for blood overcame all other thoughts and I knew that nothing would be able to reason with me now. A speedy descent across to Wooler had brought me closer to my target. The second I landed, I spread myself out to my full length as well as lying low against the rocky terrain, because I knew that my disfigured, rugged skin would easily camouflage me into the ground and make me unnoticeable unless closely inspected.

As I waited for the right time to make the killing blow, I overheard my meal having a conversation with someone else. "Oh good," I thought, "double the effort, but a bigger reward!" – but I decided to let them finish their petty little conversation (it was the least I could do considering I was just about to drain the life out of them).

"What's the matter with ye? – Hic! – Surely ye can't still be troubled about yer parents – Hic! – finding ou' that ye only got 75% in yer exam?" came a deep, obviously drunken voice from around the corner.

"No. It's not that; it's the fact that Saint George has gone ou' huntin' again. I mean, if he doesn't listen to the authorities and stop soon, we'll 'ave no wildlife left. And the rumours say that he skins the poor animals alive – and then leaves 'em to rot without putting any of the meat or skins to good use! It's horrific!" whined a tearful, high-pitched voice in answer to the previous speaker.

"I'm sure that's not true. An' anyway, why's he called 'Saint' George if he's so blooming murderous?"

"I think it's because it's ironic. A saint would never do anythin' against the way of God, but George is going around an' destroying all of the wonderful creatures that God created."

All selfish desires for the juice that ran through the veins of those people instantaneously vanished from my mind as a boiling anger rushed through me. My decision was instant: no innocent lives would be destroyed tonight, only that of a villain against nature. I took flight without worrying about keeping the humans from knowing I was there, and glided swiftly over towards the most obvious place for animal killings: Cheviot Forest (it was secluded and well hidden: perfect for committing devious deeds).

I found where I needed to be easily enough; this person they called George had left a trail of devastation behind him; a fresh trail of blood led me to a clearing where a herd of young deer were grazing nonchalantly. They clearly weren't aware of a middle-aged man slowly closing in on them with a rifle held up to his hidden face and aimed at the seemingly oldest of the pitiful herd. I quietly lurked up behind the man and wrenched his puny little head off before he had time to utter a sound; I tore George apart so ferociously that he was totally unrecognisable by the time I had finished with him. Oddly, my appetite had disappeared by then.

Feeling rather ashamed at myself for losing my temper so easily, and shocked that I had killed out of anger, I skulked back to my lonely cave to dwell on what I had just done.

Weeks later – and still feeling rather dejected – I was pleasantly surprised by a gift from the people of the surrounding villages. It was a donation of blood, to satisfy my thirst without my having to condemn any more lives to a treacherous end – and a declaration that I was their hero for saving those animals that otherwise would have had their lives wasted just for the enjoyment of an arrogant poacher. It would seem that my erstwhile meal had witnessed my outburst and spread the word.

Imagine that! Me, a hero!

By Molly Dalgleish, aged 12

With my head hanging low, I suck on my cigarette. I let the smoke steadily escape my dry, cracked lips and I watch the grey cloud disappear into the inky night sky. As I walk around Berwick, I take my time to observe the little, indistinct things that people seldom notice. The slim cracks in the pavement, which small forms of life have colonised. Weeds claw their way up from underneath the earth, bombarding the smooth walkways. Beetles and spiders have claimed their accommodation, cowering from the five-foot fiends above, trampling their homes with their large feet. Screaming and shouting, they destroy the habitats of nature's creatures.

I look up to the Town Hall. I can only faintly see the different shades of bricks that are stacked, one upon the other, up until they fade into the foggy black sky. I turn right, crossing the desolate road. I walk past the chippy, remembering the soft, yet crunchy chips I had the night before – lovely and warm in my mouth, the hint of salt and vinegar tingling on my tongue made my taste buds dance. I take a deep breath through my nose, the smell of fish and chips and kebabs still lingers around the shop at this time of night. It reminds me of the good times, when me and my friends would walk down by the river, laughing and gossiping about people we hated at school. But that was ages ago. So, so long ago. That doesn't happen any more, everyone has left me. I am alone and isolated, in my own little world of self-hate. No one even cares any more.

I walk past the Beehive. I smile at the good memories, going on trips, making films, chatting to new people. It was wonderful! But when I became lonely, I left. I spent as much time as possible locked away in my room, flicking through Facebook to see that my so-called friends were having the time of their lives together, excluding me. I don't understand what I have done. I was always there for them, whenever they were upset, I was there. But when I am sad, I'm left alone. They don't care. It took me longer than it should have to realise that they were using me. Whenever they needed comforting, and nobody was there for them, they would come crying to me. Why didn't I realise it sooner? How can I be so stupid as to think somebody actually likes me?

I look at my feet, and drop the butt of my cigarette on the ground, stamping on it to put it out. All my thoughts race around my head at the same time; it creates a blurry vision of my future, too blurry to make out. If I'm going to do this, I need to think about it. I need to think things through, how people will feel. How my dad will cope. Will he even care? I don't know... probably not. I try to file my thoughts, decide what I should think about first, leaving the most important one to last: it may change my mind.

I look up to see I'm nearly halfway across the new bridge. I reach into my pocket to pull out another cigarette and a lighter. As I light my cigarette, I notice that my hands are shaking from the sudden cold air. I had not realised it before. It's cold like death, as if the deceased have come to haunt me; or to guide me. I breathe-in the black, life-threatening smoke, not caring any more about what it'll do to me. I look over the waters, just making out the Spittal Willy. I remember, in Year Nine, we learned about it in Geography and all laughed at the bizarre name. I smile at the memory. I turn my gaze to beyond the horizon, and think about everything.

School. It isn't going great. I failed nearly all my GCSEs. I'm a failure. Yeah sure, those last few months weren't the best for me with my mum... Never mind. But I just can't cope with school any more, the amount of homework that is piled up and I just can't finish because I don't have time to. I even do it when I'm at the hospital, but the teachers just don't understand how hard it is to do with everything that is going on in my life. The stress is slowly squeezing me, making me unable to breathe. Too much stress. Too much stress! It isn't good. I wouldn't be surprised if my hair turned grey soon, it's probably starting to. It hurts, you know, all this stress. It give me headaches and migraines, horrible things they are. It doesn't make anything easier, either. I now think about my next two years in sixth form. I don't see the point in doing it anymore. I miss half my lessons, I don't understand anything. What is the point? I'm going to fail anyway. I suck on my cigarette again, watching the deadly smoke blend into the peaceful night. I turn my thoughts away from school.

Friends. Or lack thereof. One person. That's it. One person sticks by me. Don't get me wrong. I'm glad she is there, but not always. She always goes to these nights out that I'm excluded from, she has fun with them. And I'm glad she does, I would prefer it if she was with them, she can't have any fun with me, no nights out, no drinks, no movies, just misery. But she's still there for me sometimes. Maybe she'll be upset if I do move somewhere else. But she'll soon forget about me. Everyone else, though, they'll probably laugh and say: "I'm glad she's gone!" And "It's about time, eh?" And "Finally, not an annoying bitch in sight!" Tears begin to form in my eyes as I think about them. What have I done to deserve this? What have I done to be treated like a piece of shit? I don't know. I just don't know. That's it though, it's been decided. They won't care. I stub my fag out on the cold, rocky, mossy brick wall, and flick it into the river, watching it as it descends into darkness, into my grave. I grab my lighter and the half-empty packet of cigarettes and, in sudden anger and fear, I throw them into the deadly water.

Family. How will my dad feel? My brain tells me he won't care, but my heart tells me he will. And now that I think about it, I know he will. I am the only thing he has left. If I leave, he'll be devastated, he won't be able to sleep. He might leave himself. Ever since Mum… died, he has been lonely and depressed. But every time he sees me, he smiles. It hurts him, because he knows he may lose me. But he remembers her. He looks at my blue eyes, my freckles, my brown hair, and thinks about the wonderful gift his wife gave him. He would pull me into a hug and say, "Look, everything's going to be alright, I have faith in you. Hope. And hope is the strongest magic of all." Then we'd laugh a little about his comment. Magic. We need magic. Not Harry Potter-like magic, although that would be cool. More like medieval magic. Magic that can heal anything. Magic that can bring people back from the dead who didn't deserve to die.

Mum. Tears roll down my cheeks as I think about her. I remember the features of her face perfectly, like she's standing in front of me. Her golden brown hair, so light it flows behind her like a cape in the slightest breeze. Her ocean blue eyes, that reflect the sparkling sea in the most beautiful way. The way her eyes crease slightly as she smiles, the dimples that form on her cheeks. Her smile: it made everyone else around her smile too. The light freckles dotted across her cheeks and nose, they bloom in the summer. Her perfect posture, everything about her is wonderful. She is so kind to everyone, not a single sign of hate. Even when she was on her deathbed, she said: "They were just teens, it's what they do, darling. It's okay, I forgive them. I'm happy. I need you and Dad to move on, be happy. Never stop being happy." More tears race down my cheeks, speeding, like those boys who killed her. They were devastated, of course, they couldn't live with themselves. They were speeding slightly round a corner, and didn't see her. They hit her and the blood... it was too much, they said. A lot of blood. A lot of death and blood and horror and darkness and pain and sorrow. And death. She's gone. My sobs are silent no longer. I put my head in my hands and cry. My first proper cry since Mum died. It kinda feels good to let it all out. I take in deep breaths, to try and calm myself, and shift my thoughts to something horrible.

Cancer. A few months before Mum died, I was diagnosed with breast cancer. The thing is, when Mum was there by my side, I wasn't scared. She said she'll always be there with me, that there is no need to be afraid because she'll protect me. But now she's gone, I want to give up. All this treatment, all these doctors' appointments and hospitals and scans. They are horrible, torturous without her. She protected me from the demons of cancer, but now she's gone. I'm too scared to have an operation. I can't do it. Not without Mum. I want to give up on treatment. It's too painful, too stressful. It makes me sick. I wipe away the warm tears that have trickled down my pale skin like a waterfall. Dad will be upset. I need to have treatment for him. But it's too much for me, he knows that. I just... I can't. I close my eyes and breathe-in the cold, salty air. I climb up the wall and stand on it, brushing the loose bits of rock and stone off my hands. I find it difficult to shift my thoughts to the most important thing.

The last one... the last thought.

Suicide. As I look down at the cold, dark, murderous river below, the soft sounds of the waves lapping pierce my ears. Everything in my life is going wrong. Everything I do is wrong. I can't do anything. I can't concentrate on my schoolwork; I can't have the operation to hopefully rid me of my deathly cancer; I can't eat; I can't sleep; I can't make friends; I can't stop them from leaving me; I can't make my dad proud; I can't live. What is the point in being alive in this world, when the time you're in it, you can't actually live? If I just jump off of the edge and land in the water it'll be painless, right? That's what people say, don't they? I will jump, and I will be gone, I will have moved, I won't be in the way any more. People won't care. They won't notice that I'm gone. Dad will get over me and I can see Mum again. Then when I die, I can be happy…

Suddenly, my thoughts turn back to my family. Mum… she won't be proud. She will be happy to see me, but she won't. I've ruined my dad's life, her love's life. She wants us to move on and we need to do that. If I'm gone, Dad will go to. We won't be happy. We will miss the McDonald's burgers we have every so often. We will miss the TV shows we would watch and laugh and cry at together. We would miss classic Jeremy Kyle. If I'm alive, I can be happy. Dad makes me happy. And maybe I'll find someone who'll make me happy and we can have children and Dad will have grandchildren and… and we'll be happy. My mum is with me. She's in my heart, she'll always be watching over me. I will have my operation, with my dad by my side and Mum in our hearts. I will be okay, I will be happy.

I've been so stupid, so, so stupid. How could I have even thought about something like that? Right now, we might be miserable, but there's years and years ahead of us. That time is the time to be happy. I have so long, and I didn't even know it. I climb off of the wall and begin to run home, tears staining my cheeks. It's only now that I realise, with the sharp, cold wind blowing against my face, that I was on the edge of both life and death. It could have gone either way, but I chose the better option, the happier option. And I don't regret a thing.

I was on the edge of death, and it was horrible. It was death itself.

By Aimee Southwood

The contributors

ANDREW AYRE, a resident of Tweedmouth, founded the Wilson's Tales Project in 2013 to celebrate and revive interest in *Wilson's Tales* and some of the local stories and heritage embedded in them.

He first became aware of the Tales as a child, when the title was given to someone to perform as a New Year charade. Now an accountant by profession, he has maintained a keen interest in history, literature and local events. He is currently reading his way through the Tales and researching for future events, publications and talks.

www.wilsonstales.co.uk

DENISE BRADSHAW was born, brought up and educated in Berwick-upon-Tweed. Lucky enough to have her interest in reading and literature nurtured by Derek Butler when studying English at Berwick High School, she has never stopped loving words, stories or language since then. Using the techniques of good storytellers, she continues to present case facts and relevant circumstances effectively in her work as a lawyer. Now living in Ipswich and working mainly in the British Indian Ocean, she still loves returning home to Berwick to spend time with family, touch base with her roots and regroup.

MICHAEL FENTY is a retired GP living in Coldingham. He has been writing for many years, initially articles for medical magazines and later, after retirement, drama.

Michael's play *The Resurrection Man*, based on the letters and trial documents of local doctor George Laurie, tried in 1820 for grave robbing, was performed by the New Strides Theatre Company; and in 2013 he contributed four short plays to a dramatised walk in the Lammermuirs, *The Footsteps of Flodden*. In 2016, his play *Tibbie Tamson* was performed by the Borders Youth Theatre

The Royal Raid and *The Monks of Dryburgh* were his first two dramatisations for Wilson's Tales. His next, *The Monomaniac*, was performed at Paxton House in 2014 and can be seen on YouTube at **www.youtube.com/watch?v=Yps8-uo8RD4&feature=youtu.b**

Michael's blog *Gangril Days* is at **http://gangrildays.blogspot.co.uk/**

NICK JONES spent many years in Cumbria's Eden Valley milling organic stoneground flour and organising arts projects. Now he lives on a windswept hill overlooking Tweed and Lammermuirs, writing stories about rubbish and railways, reviewing exhibitions for *Artwork*, drawing, painting and learning to play the piano.

nicolasjbjones@gmail.com   www.jonesnick@wordpress.com

MARY KENNY is a storyteller living in Innerleithen. Her repertoire of tales is broad and deep, but includes a special love for the stories and ballads of the Borderlands. A visual artist for 35 years, with work in public and private collections at home and abroad, Mary has a workshop in the grounds of Traquair House. She also sings with Borders-based a cappella group The Fisher Lassies.

"As an oral storyteller," she says, "the challenge of working with this extraordinary, encyclopaedic collection of tales is to adapt what can be a flowery and outmoded style of written language, and re-interpret the story sensitively for a new audience".

www.marykenny.co.uk

JOE LANG began his writing career as a journalist, playwright and advertising copywriter. He started a London-based communications consultancy business, which he ran for 30 years before moving to Berwick and rediscovering the joys of freelance life.

joe@kaineslang.com

FORDYCE MAXWELL, oldest of a family of nine from Cramond Hill Farm, Cornhill on Tweed, was educated at Berwick Grammar School and Harper Adams Agricultural College. He has been a journalist since 1967. Much of that time was with *The Scotsman* as agricultural and rural affairs editor, columnist, diarist, Parliamentary sketch writer, feature writer, leader writer and book reviewer. He has freelanced for many other newspapers and magazines and continues to do so, including as Halidon in the Tweeddale Press. He has received the MBE for services to journalism and the Scottish Newspaper Editors' award for lifetime achievement.

CHARLES NASMYTH is an artist and illustrator who has also been an art master at Stewart's Melville College in Edinburgh for many years. He is known for his illustrative work and painting based on the lives and poetry of Robert Burns and William McGonagall. His images have regularly featured in *Edinburgh Life* magazine and the *World Burns Chronicle*, and 2007 saw the publication of his graphic novel *The Comic Legend of William McGonagall* (Waverley Books).

www.nasmyth.org.uk

KEITH RYAN was born on the right side of the Tweed at Castle Hills Maternity Home and educated at Berwick Grammar School. He is a solicitor by trade, historian by nature, and Lisbon Lion in his dreams. Author of *Bloody Berwick*, a history of the town when it stood centre stage in three centuries of Anglo-Scottish medieval warfare, he has his boots by his bed for when the call comes from Celtic Park.

keithryan3@aol.com   www.bloodyberwick.com